With Best Compliments from:

Ekta Book Company
Shop No.-2, Lawyers Chambers Block-I,
Next to UCO Bank A.T.M., Delhi High Court,
Sher Shah Road, New Delhi - 110003
Tel. : 23388588, 23383875 Telefax : 23383334

About the author

The author writes fiction founded on facts, the facts being cases that he conducted as a young barrister acting for defendants charged with various crimes and appearing to answer them at the Central Criminal Court in London, the Old Bailey. Derek Wheatley went on to become a Recorder of the Crown Court before going into the City as Chief Legal Adviser at Lloyds Bank.

It is not for the barrister to reach his own decision as to the guilt or innocence of his client, but to accept his instructions and to secure the best result that he can for his client, while keeping strictly within the Rule of Law and the etiquette of his profession. And so it was with Tam Pearse. The one exception has nothing to do with courts of law and relates to a family holiday on the beach at Sangenjo in North West Spain and the strange encounter of a young happy family man with an unknown, mysterious, aristocratic lady.

By the same author

The Silent Lady – Mona Lisa, (Vanguard Press), 2008
ISBN 978 1843864 257

Brief Encounters

Derek Wheatley

Brief Encounters

FIRST INDIAN REPRINT, 2012

Universal
Law Publishing Co. Pvt. Ltd.
NEW DELHI - INDIA

First Indian Reprint, 2012

ISBN : 978-93-5035-205-2

Published by
UNIVERSAL LAW PUBLISHING CO. PVT. LTD.
C-FF-1A, Dilkhush Industrial Estate,
(Near Azadpur Metro Station) G.T. Karnal Road,
Delhi-110 033
Tel.: 011-47082254, 27438103, 27215334
Fax : 011-27458529
E-mail *(For sales inquiries)* : unilaw@vsnl.com
Website : www.unilawbooks.com

Under special arrangement with
Pegasus Elliot Mackenzie Publishers Ltd., UK

A CIP catalogue record for this title is
available from the British Library

For Sale in Indian Sub-continent only.

Printed in India at Sita Fine Arts Pvt. Ltd., New Delhi.

Silence in Court

'Where shall I begin, please your Majesty?
he asked,
'Begin at the beginning', the King
said gravely, 'and go on till you
come to the end: then stop'

Alice in Wonderland
Lewis Carroll

Tam Pearse began his army career in the pleasantest fashion, considering that, although he was only 18, there was a war on with Germany, and D-Day (the invasion of Europe), had still to come. He was sent on a 'short university course' to Oxford University. At the time, it was thought that he was 'Officer Material' and that it was really a very good way of extending his experience, and turning him into a better officer if he spent six months in the city of 'dreaming spires', learning from university dons about things that certainly *might* be useful to his army career, as well as spending two days a week with the Oxford University Training Corps doing effectively the same basic army training that he would be doing over and over again, when he passed on to the army proper after the university short course was over. In fact he was not to pass out as an officer, having completed all the training, until after Victory Europe (VE) Day when the war

11

was finally over and the occupation of Germany, with its long period of restitution, began. His time in the British Army of the Rhine was spent in occupying the conquered enemy, rather than in actual fighting. However, time passed pleasantly enough for him as a young subaltern, a cornet of horse, in Lingen in North Germany where the 8th Kings Royal Irish Hussars were stationed.

And why this particular regiment you may ask? Well Tam Pearse had no Irish blood in him as far as he knew; although he knew that there was a faint link in the past between some ancestor of his and one Padraig Pearse, who had played an important part in Ireland in 1916 by standing on the steps of the Post Office in Dublin, shouting defiance to the English and precipitating the start of 'The Troubles' with the Black and Tans in that country. The real reason was that his good friend, Tim O'Malley, was Irish, and had been accepted for a place in the regiment when he passed out from Sandhurst, and had shown Tam some photographs of the uniform, which had yellow stripes down the trouser legs of the 'Mess Overalls' and chain mail on the shoulders. It all looked very dashing and calculated to help a lot in winning the hearts of a large number of fair young ladies... at least Tam thought so. But war or no war, a regiment such as the Kings Royal Irish Hussars had to be careful that its officers were suitable material for such a famous regiment. After all it had been one of the six cavalry regiments that formed the Light Brigade which had charged so famously, if futilely, 'into the valley of death' at the Battle of Balaclava. And so it was that before passing out from Sandhurst as an officer, Tam was required to attend the Colonel-in-Chief of his chosen regiment in London and was provided with a day off from officer training for the purpose.

The interview took place in the Cavalry Club where Tam, freshly shaved and wearing his best battledress, with the white tabs of an Officer Cadet on the lapels, found General Sir Humphry Harrington sitting in a private room. Sir

Humphry was all charm and offered Tam a cup of coffee to put him at his ease. But there was a serious matter to be discussed, even though, or perhaps particularly because, there was a war going on.

'Where did you go to school, young man?' was the question which began the interview and the answer seemed to please the General

'Good rugger-playing school, that...! but do ye ride?'

'Yes, Sir Humphry, I enjoy riding,' said Tam, truthfully, although he did not elaborate on the few occasions that he had managed to go for a short hack on a horse at his local stables.

'But do ye hunt?'

Truthfully, but hesitatingly, Tam admitted that he did not hunt.

'Never mind; plenty of time for that now that the War is over.'

And the interview concluded with the General's assurance that all that Tam had to do was to pass out from Sandhurst, and a place as an officer in that famous regiment would be his. And pass out as an officer he did, and enjoyed his time in the British Army of the Rhine, where his regiment was stationed at the German town of Lingen in North Germany. But his life was still before him and he had a career to make, since he did not see himself as a career professional soldier. There had been no doubt about his going into the forces at eighteen. There was a war on. Now it was over and he had a career to make, and he decided that it was to be as a barrister.

Not that there had ever been any barristers in the Pearse family tree. The Pearses had been squires, farmers, Methodist ministers, landowners, even bankers but never lawyers; so it was a big departure. But Tam had read about Sir Edward Marshal Hall, the great defender of Victorian times, who had obtained the most improbable of acquittals in the cases where the prosecution's case had seemed the most unanswerable. His imagination had been fired. If Sir Edward had been able to do it then why shouldn't Tam Pearse have a damned good try at doing the same? He saw himself defending a case of life or death for his client, innocent, however black his or her case had seemed, in the great criminal courts. Like Sir Edward, he would find the one answer no one else had even thought about. And he would be able to make it stick. But, at the moment, he was in Lingen and the Law Courts were far away indeed. He did have a demob number which was due to come up in about a year's time. Next term at Oxford was due to start in October and he had been promised at place at University College, where he had done his six months' short course, if he could get there. There was just a very slim chance he might be able to get a special early release. He thought that it just worth a try if he had the colonel of the regiment on his side.

Lt-Colonel Cuthbert Dromgoole was the colonel of the KRI Hussars. His brother, Eddie, was a brigadier in the Guards. Cuthie, as everyone knew him, was a large man who looked very good on a horse, with his enormous cavalry moustache, his boots and his spurs. He had been with his dearly beloved regiment since the days of peace, and had become a very good tank commander in the Libyan desert when the regiment became 'Desert Rats', part of the 8th Armoured Division under General Montgomery. Peace had meant a return to the great love of his life, horses and the life of a peacetime soldier once more. He was a very good colonel and recognised Tam Pearse as something a bit different from himself; being a soldier for 'hostilities only', rather than the very professional soldier he was himself. It was with some trepidation that Tam sought an interview with him to share his problem.

14

'So you've had a promise that Oxford will take you back in October so you can learn to be a lawyer, young feller?'

'Yes, Colonel, I've loved my life in the regiment but I do feel I've got to get on with my life. I don't see myself as a professional soldier, only a wartime one. I'm war-substantive as a lieutenant now, but that is not of course the same as a regular commission and frankly I think that this is a great career but I don't think it's for me. The problem is that my demob number is too high for the usual Class A release, which is only likely to come up next summer and too late for my promised place. Would I have your *approval* if I were to apply for a special Class B release, for exceptional reasons, which might get me back in time?'

Colonel Cuthie agreed and so it was that Tam Pearse made a start to his career as a barrister, delayed only by the three and a half years he had served in the army as a wartime soldier. And then it meant life again at Oxford. The amazing thing was, that Tam did actually learn quite a lot about the law, lectures and tutorials being given pride of place among the much more enjoyable social life of an undergraduate. It all seemed a bit of a time warp to Tam. A short time before he had been someone quite important in an armoured regiment. He had risen to command a troop of armoured cars, including a number of captured German and even Italian vehicles. Now, the strict rules of Oxford in 1946 meant that he was not even allowed to have a drink in a pub without the risk of it being raided by a patrolling proctor and his 'bull-dogs', the University servants dressed in sober dark clothes and bowler hats who came behind him, to do his bidding: to pursue and apprehend any recalcitrant undergraduate found to be committing the offence of being caught drinking in a pub. In 1946, undergraduates were not meant to go into pubs and risked the wrath of the College authority, the Dean, if they were caught doing so. But it was a small price to pay and meant that life was still full of excitement; because, of course, Tam did take a chance now and again. The forbidden fruit of

15

a pint in the King's Arms was well worth the risk, and was somehow even more welcome as refreshment because of the very real danger that he might have to escape hurriedly by the back door as the bulldogs came in at the front.

Life at Oxford was soon followed by life in London doing his Bar exams and the final triumph of being 'called to the Bar' and the early years as a young man in chambers in The Temple. For the young barrister, briefs are essential so that he can get going in his profession. But how to get them when none of the solicitors had ever heard of him? Well the system works through that important being, the barrister's clerk; in Tam's case in his new chambers at 6, Damson Court, The Temple, this was Challen. For reasons unknown, he was never known to members of the chambers by his Christian name. He must have had one, but nobody knew what it was. He was never spoken of as 'Mr Challen', except by the respectful solicitors and their clerks who came to chambers with their briefs and their clients. He was a sometime Mayor of Brighton, suave with the appearance and manners of an avuncular butler; he started the young men on their way with a brief that was delivered for some other member of the same chambers, who found that he could not do it after all because, perhaps, some other case of his had overrun its expected duration.

Tam had become a substitute on several occasions. Sometimes he did the case well and the solicitor concerned was impressed enough to send him some briefs on his own account. But it was a slow business at first and meant doing criminal cases, which were more plentiful than anything else, since they tended to be less well paid than civil disputes involving large sums of money. Tam only started to do the better paid work because he realised that money mattered and that any case had got its own interest. But to begin with, Tam was still fresh from the army and any kind of work was scarce for the newly-called young barrister. However the astute Challen, playing upon Tam's recent experience as a wartime soldier, managed to get his name down for work from the Director of Army Legal Services defending at courts martial in Germany, where the British still had large numbers of troops occupying that defeated country.

It was a novel experience for Tam when he got the brief to defend Warrant Officer Edworthy at a court martial in Hamburg. He was provided with an 'equivalent' army rank, which was no less than that of colonel. It was quite a promotion, he reflected, since he had never been anything higher than a subaltern when serving with the 8th KRI Hussars. It meant that he had a cabin to himself on the boat from Harwich to the Hook of Holland. It meant that he found himself in a first class compartment of a train to Hamburg. He was sharing it with a brigadier and two full colonels who were en route to rejoin their units in the British Army of the Rhine. Each one was immersed in the pages of their copies of *The Times*, when Tam rather nervously took his seat. They lowered the pages of their papers to inspect the young man in civilian clothes who had come to join them. What they made of him he could only guess, but they were soon immersed once more in the columns devoted to army promotions and the cricket scores.

Then there came the moment when Tam experienced a call of nature and went off to find the toilet on the bucketing train. His mission completed he looked up to pull the chain. Yes, there it was, above his head. It did not look very familiar, but it must be the right one because it was the only one he could see, so pull the brass handle coming down from the roof, he did. But what had he done? He looked up to see that there were words in red in Dutch, or was it German? alongside the handle he had pulled; perhaps they were giving some warning? The train started to come to a long drawn out, shuddering halt. It had been travelling at full speed so that by the time it was finally motionless, Tam had managed to find the right handle to pull to evacuate the bowl of the WC at last and was back in his seat among his three companions. When

17

finally at rest, there was the noise of railwaymen coming along outside the train, tapping at the wheels. Then officials came down the corridor and opened each door, making enquiries apparently, but in German, or was it Dutch? and quite incomprehensible to Tam. Or, he suspected, to any of the three senior officers, who now lowered their copies of *The Times* briefly to stare in silent disapproval at their interrogators. Tam lowered his own copy of the paper, looked apparently with equal incomprehension at the uniformed train guards and remained as silent as his companions. Of course he could have, perhaps he should have, tried to explain that he had been the unwitting cause of it all? Somehow he shirked the difficulties any kind of explanation would have been bound to entail. Had he been a coward, or had he merely been following the old adage that 'Discretion is the better part of valour'? He often wondered.

Tam was met on arrival and escorted to the regimental depot where the alleged offence was said to have been committed. He had already read the papers in the case and knew that W.O. Edworthy was accused of having wrongly obtained the sum of £430 by false entries in the books under his control, which credited that sum to him. He might have noticed those entries, particularly since they were in his own favour, but he simply had not done so. He did not actually say that one does not question gifts from the gods. He just had not noticed and, if he had, why then he would have put the whole matter right, of course. It all seemed a pretty shaky defence to Tam, but he had no option other than to put it forward as best he could. He reminded himself that it was for the prosecution to prove W.O. Edworthy guilty and not for him to prove him innocent, and that there was, after all, no direct evidence as to who had made the mistake since anyone in the paymaster's office might have done so. According to Edworthy, there were several people in his office who might have born a grudge against him, but he was quite unclear about any details and did not wish to accuse anyone in particular.

Tam was provided with the services of an 'assistant defending officer, but the young man concerned seemed to take a very gloomy view of there being any chance of success for the unfortunate Edworthy who was likely to be discharged from the army without a pension if found to be guilty. Edworthy in any event, stoutly affirmed that he was not guilty so that Tam had no choice except to do the best he could. Luckily the army accounting system was far from perfect and when the case came on for trial, Tam spent a lot of time in cross-examining the prosecution witnesses and putting holes in the system of that particular regimental pay-office, without quite being able to expose any flaw which, by itself, could have invalidated the case against his client.

Courts martial are presided over by a senior officer and, in this case, it was a Colonel Thornton, who sat in the middle of four other officers with the judge advocate, the Honourable Robert Acland-Drake next to him, when Tam came into court on the first day of the case. He had already read his brief through several times; he had already conferred with his client and his 'junior counsel'. None of it had got him very far in deciding how to get the lugubrious looking Warrant Officer Edworthy off the hook. To make matters worse, his client had told him that he was going to exercise his undoubted right not to give evidence on his own account. That meant that he would not be subject to the hostile cross-examination of the prosecution as to who could have forged the paymaster's signatures, if it had not been him, when after all, he accepted that the missing money had found its way into his personal account. Some mistake must have been made and he agreed that he should pay the money back. Well that was all to his advantage as a mitigating factor, but was hardly going to help him from answering the charges made against him.

'Who could it possibly have been then? Surely it must have been someone in your own department, if it was not you?' Tam had asked him several times. But W.O. Edworthy

19

could not say; 'Someone who had a grudge against me' was his best guess, 'I've made a few enemies in my own department.'

It was true that the whole affair had come to light because of an anonymous tip-off in an unsigned note addressed to the adjutant of the regiment, who had felt bound to put the matter into the hands of the Royal Military Police for their investigation, which had resulted in this trial. Colonel Thornton, the President of the Court, had to defer to the judge advocate on all matters of law and his whole manner made it plain that he did not much like deferring on anything to anyone. He liked to run things in his own court, as he liked to run things in his own regiment. But the court, of course, had no option but to accept the legal advice provided by the judge advocate, who was a lawyer, whose function was to decide all legal issues that came before the court, as well as to provide the usual functions of a judge by summing up the evidence that was put before the court. But Colonel Thornton was the President of the Court. He seemed to have little regard for any of the lawyers but, of course, he had to conform to the practice and listen with at least apparent respect to what they had to say.

Warrant Officer Edworthy had told Tam that he resolutely refused to give evidence and neither Tam nor anyone else could force him to do so, although Tam had strongly advised him that he should because otherwise it looked very much as if he was afraid of being cross-examined about the forged entries made in his favour. There was just one chance that Tam could conceal the fact that Edworthy was not going to give any evidence in his own defence. If Tam could make a submission of 'no case to answer' at the end of the prosecution case, then there would be no need for any evidence from the defendant or from anyone else on his behalf, because that would be the end of the matter and would result in Edworthy's triumphal acquittal. Tam began to convince himself that a submission of 'no case to answer'

20

might well succeed. After all, there was no direct evidence that Edworthy had made the typed false entries in his own favour. His own failure to notice and to correct them might well have been the reason he refused to give evidence on oath so that he could be questioned about that failure. But first, the prosecution had to prove their case against him.

And so it was that as soon as the last formal prosecution witness had give given evidence Tam was on his feet making an impassioned plea that his client, a man of excellent good character and high standing in the army, who had at once repaid the whole of the money, once the mistake had been pointed out to him, had no case to answer and should have the case against him dismissed at once. As Tam made this impassioned plea he looked up at the court. All the officers were listening intently, although it was now after lunch and, as he had experienced himself in the officers' mess, wine was served at lunch. He noticed now that the judge advocate had his head on his arms on the desk in front of him, but he could not see his eyes. Could it possibly be that he was asleep? And then Tam saw Colonel Thornton apparently give him a nudge, so that he at once sat bolt upright and gave his ruling on the submission that had just been made to him. Not very much to Tam Pearse's surprise, the very short ruling that followed was that there was a case to answer. But Tam was in the greatest difficulty because he had no evidence to call. W.O. Edworthy refused to give any evidence himself; he had no witnesses to call, since there was nobody in his own department, which was the only one which had been concerned, who could, or who was prepared to give any evidence on his behalf. It had come across to Tam before that W.O. Edworthy was perhaps not the most popular of men in the regiment he served.

So all that Tam could do was to say very much the same as he had said before: there was no proof that Edworthy's had been the hand which had altered the ledger so as to show pay due to him, which was so very much above that which it

21

should have been because of the two fictitious entries. Edworthy accepted that they were fictitious. He had paid the money back. But if he had not made those entries, which Tam had to accept that he had had every opportunity to do, then who had? Well it was not for the defence in this case, or in any other, to provide the answer to that question because if there was any doubt in the matter, then Edworthy was fully entitled to the benefit of that doubt. Tam finished his impassioned address, which he made as etiquette demanded after the prosecuting officer, Captain Smiley, had had his own say. And they all withdrew from the court allowing the members of it to consider their verdict.

Tam and his opposite number a captain in the Directorate of Army Legal Services, were left to chat to each other outside. As often happened they got on very well together and agreed to spend that night, since Tam was not due to return to England until later the next day, exploring the high lights of Hamburg. There was the Reeperbahn, the nightclub area to be explored. If they went together, they would surely come to no harm. They decided that they would have a glance, but no more, at the Winklestrasse where the local ladies of the town were reputed to display their wares in shop windows, wearing not very much in the way of clothes, and perhaps a nightclub or two in the famous Reeperbahn. If they stayed together and ended up at Tam's hotel, they could not come to much harm and it might be good, fairly clean fun. And so it proved, although not without its surprises.

But then the orderly came out of the closed doors of the courtroom to say that everyone should return as the court was agreed upon its verdict. W.O. Edworthy was brought in to sit in his place once more, flanked by an escorting colleague of equal rank. All eyes turned at once to a small table set in front of the court and before the eyes of the prisoner. Upon it was his sword which had stood there since the beginning of the trial, placed sideways. If the result of all the court's deliberations had been an acquittal, then the hilt would have been facing towards him, as an early indication that he might take it up and put it round his waist, as he resumed his important duties in the army. But the hilt was placed away from him and the scabbard, with the naked blade inside, pointed straight towards him.

The day's formalities were concluded by the President passing sentence upon him for fraud and embezzlement, which was that he be dismissed from the service without a pension. So, Tam Pearse's very first venture into courts martial was hardly a successful one. But Tam was not easily dismayed. He saw his client and discussed the possibility that he might appeal the decision of the court to the newly formed Court of Courts Martial Appeals, which was a branch of the High Court of Justice and presided over by the Lord Chief Justice himself. But what were the grounds for making any such appeal? Well, Tam thought he could come up with several. The first of them was the sheer fact that there had been no proof, only surmise based upon the undoubted fact that the only one to benefit from the frauds had been the accused man himself. The rest was all assumption. Or so Tam told himself as he set to work on drafting the grounds of appeal, which he did after a consultation with his client, and as soon as he had returned to Damson Court in The Temple.

Tam was able to think of a number of quite convincing-looking grounds of appeal. There had been the singular lack of any direct evidence that W.O. Edworthy had been the one to falsify the entries in his favour. Would he really have been such a fool as to risk his entire army career, so far so distinguished, for such a sum of money? When questioned about the matter by the Royal Military Police, he had steadfastly denied any knowledge of it and, as soon as it was pointed out to him, he had paid the money back straight away. Some of the evidence adduced by the prosecution was of doubtful validity and Tam made that the subject of several of the counts in his grounds of appeal. He hardly liked to include the highly improbable ground of appeal that the judge advocate, who should have been giving his closest attention to the serious case being tried before him, had instead appeared to be dropping off to sleep and, once at least, actually looked to be asleep. After all, it was not for counsel for the accused to give evidence to the Court of Courts Martial Appeals. Fresh evidence would have had to be called to establish such an unlikely thing, which would have been likely to jeopardise the whole career of the judge advocate in question. Tam almost left it out, so slender did his prospects of success on that point seem, and how difficult it would be for him even to raise it in the absence of any admissible evidence about it. But his was not a craven heart and he did put it in as Ground Number 10: 'The judge advocate appeared to give little attention to arguments put before him by the defence and, at one stage, appeared to be paying no attention to them and to be asleep.' Of course, it did not follow that he had to develop that particular ground of appeal and, with any reasonable luck, one or more of the others would find favour with the court so that he would not have to.

On the day that W.O. Edworthy's appeal was heard, Tam Pearse was taken over from 6 Damson Court, with Challen himself carrying his blue bag containing his wig and robes. He had to wait his turn while other cases were heard and then, at last, he was on his feet addressing that distinguished court with Lord Parker, the Lord Chief Justice himself, presiding. He did his very best to make the several points in his lengthy Notice of Appeal. The court dealt with them all with extremely short shrift, Lord Parker saying:

'Mr Pearse, we've listened very carefully to all you have had to say but at the end of the day, it is surely all a question of fact. In most criminal cases this would be for the jury to decide, but in the case of a court martial, it is for the court itself to make that decision. And decide it has. It is hardly for this court to question that decision, and all that you have said so far does not incline us to do so... however, you have not touched on Ground 10 in your Notice of Appeal?'

'M'Lud, I do not regard it as my best point. I am in no position to call any evidence in support of it...'

'Well then, Mr Pearse, I think that you had better have a look at this letter which has been received by the court, and which has just been passed to me by the Clerk of the Court.'

And the Lord Chief Justice passed down a letter which Tam read with astonishment. He had never heard of such a thing happening in a Court of Appeal before. It was written on the letter heading of The Rifle Brigade (one of the two Green Jacket regiments), which Tam remembered was the distinguished regiment commanded by Colonel Thornton, who had been the presiding officer at the trial. It read:

'With reference to the case of Warrant Officer Henry Edworthy; I was the presiding officer at the trial of this warrant officer and none of the court was left in any doubt as to his guilt. However, I have read the Grounds of Appeal lodged in respect of him and feel duty bound to write this letter to the Court of Appeal to say that as far as Ground 10 is concerned at least, it is quite correct. The judge advocate in question did indeed nod off, apparently asleep, as that notice states. However, do not be concerned about this as the court paid little attention to what he said...'

Well that was that. If the court martial paid no attention to what the judge advocate told them, then that was good enough to ensure that the appeal succeeded on its own.

Tam Pearse said, 'M'Lud, I say no more, in view of the letter to the court that your Lordship has been good enough to show me, but ask at once that the court should allow this appeal.'

The Lord Chief Justice glanced either side of him at his fellow members of the court and said at once, 'This appeal is allowed and I see no reason to go into the court's exact reasons for its decision, having regard to the unusual circumstances of the matter which have just been disclosed.'

And so it was that W.O. Edworthy was cleared of all the charges against him and Tam Pearse won his first case in the Court of Appeal. It was also to help his reputation, since the press had been in court and next day the newspapers were full of the case, a well-known daily blazoning the headline, 'Army judge given nudge'. It left Tam wondering. He had very nearly failed to take the one point on which he eventually won the case. In future, he must take every single point which was open to him.

The Terrible Turk

'Two households, both alike in dignity,
In fair Verona, where we lay our scene
From ancient grudge break to new mutiny,
Where civil blood makes civil hands unclean...'

Romeo and Juliet
by William Shakespeare

A most important man in the life of any young barrister is his
clerk. They were characters to a man, because in the early
days when Tam Pearse started as a barrister there were
certainly no women clerks, and for that matter, very few
women barristers either. A barrister clerk's only training
would have been in the hard school of experience. There was
no formal instruction for them. Starting as the boy in
chambers, a general dogsbody charged with such menial
tasks as carrying the law books of their members of chambers
cheerfully over to court, making and taking round endless tea
for members of chambers, and clients when they came for a
conference, they would work up in time, they hoped, to the
dignity of chief clerk to a set of chambers. All the drudgery
was worth it for the ultimate prize. As senior clerks, they
became men of power. Men with the ability to make, and

some said also to break, a young man starting off in a new professional career. Older ones, too, would be subject to the influence of their chief clerk. But not to the same extent since, as time passes, every barrister starts to accumulate a list of clients of his very own. To begin with he has none, or perhaps, if he is very lucky, just one or two clients who are family connections in the solicitor's profession. So the novice is dependent, for the start upon his new professional career, upon his clerk. It is he who has the task of distributing the work that comes into all sets of chambers, without being assigned to any specific member of it. Later, as success starts to come, there will be those who have sat in court and listened to and admired his forensic skills leading to a successful conclusion for his client. Or those who have heard of some notable success he has had for another firm of solicitors. Or those who have seen his name appear in a similar case to theirs in the official law reports. Or some who just come knocking at the door, perhaps even by mistake. Tam Pearse once acquired an important client who had sent him the original brief, he later discovered, by mistake for someone else of the same name. But Tam had managed to impress him enough for him to come again and to turn into a very valued client.

Not only is there power for the senior clerk, there is also the important fact that he is entitled to a percentage of the gross fees on the work done by all the barristers in his chambers. They are men of character: men of means. One clerk in The Temple, where about half of all barristers live and move and have their being, had become Mayor of Brighton. They were men to be reckoned with. The main requirement made of them was simply to obtain the briefs necessary for everyone in The Temple to live, some of them to live very well. This meant, for many clerks at least, that they spent a great deal of time in the Devereaux, El Vino's, the Wig and Pen Club, or one or other of the numerous hostelries in Fleet Street and The Strand near to The Temple and the Royal Courts of Justice, the barristers' principal places of working and practising their skills in the courts. There they would meet up with their cronies, the solicitors' court clerks. Without exception they all seemed to be men with extraordinary thirsts, who would discuss racecourse form, the chances of Arsenal or Chelsea of winning the Cup. And many other matters of importance... and, perhaps hand over a brief before the drinks were finished.

Tam Pearse was lucky at 6, Damson Court, where he had found a 'seat' or tenancy, from which to practise the law and attempt to make a hard-earned living. G.L. Hardie was the head of chambers. Tam never discovered what the G or the L stood for since he was always just known, simply as 'G.L.' or as 'Hardie' to his colleagues. Or 'Policeman Hardie' to everyone else. Particularly to the criminal fraternity he represented in the courts, for his practice lay entirely there. The nickname was based on his considerable reputation for winning acquittals in seemingly hopeless cases. These were usually based upon a successful attack on some unfortunate police officer whose evidence was vital for the success of the prosecution. His success rate and, who knows, perhaps too his ability now and then to make the police look a bit silly, endeared him to his clients and his practice flourished. It had become Hardie's habit always to address the police witnesses as 'Policeman', regardless of their names or rank in the Force.

None of this made him any too popular with the judges. It was, after all, their duty to see that justice was done, having regard to the evidence in each case. Honesty compelled Tam to admit that in his own, still comparatively short experience, more often than not it was a 'true bill' brought against the defendant... but could the prosecution prove it? Because if not, if there were to be any real doubt about the matter, it was the task of the defence to procure an acquittal. The story was told of the case in which Hardy was appearing before an irascible judge. The principal prosecution witness had recently received rapid promotion to superintendent, but

Hardie, in accordance with his custom, referred to him in his usual way.

'Now, Policeman, had you only just come on duty moments before the incident in question?' At last the judge could stand it no longer.

'Really, Mr Hardie,' he interjected, when the impatient tapping of his pencil on his desk produced no effect, '...can you not be a little more precise? This witness is a superintendent of the police... surely... you can address him as such?'

'M'Lud,' said Hardie... 'He has been called "Sergeant" and he has been called "Inspector". On the depositions he is referred to as "Chief Inspector", now Your Lordship says he is a superintendent... it is all a bit confusing for the jury who have to be certain... but the one thing that seems clear is that he is a policeman...'

'Now, Policeman... you had just come on duty?'

Tam Pearse's clerk at 6, Damson Court, Challen, on a bright Tuesday morning in May came into Tam's room with, unmistakeably, a large fat brief, tied with the regulation red ribbon in his hands. He put it down on Tam's desk with all the reverence and ceremony of an arch-druid placing the sacrificial offering in front of the officiating priest. As always he was soberly dressed in a neat three-piece suit. His manner and bearing gave him the appearance of a rather self-indulgent bishop from a country diocese.

'Have a look at these papers please, Mr Pearse. It's for Mr Birley of Fearnley Davies and Co of Walworth. He wanted Mr Hardie to do it for him but his case down at Lewes is likely to run over into next week, so I persuaded Mr Birley that you are just the man for the job. It's down at the Bailey and could be in the list for Thursday. I've got Mr Birley to come in with his client at 4.30 so you'd better have a look at the papers right away. It's an "attempted murder", and I don't think it looks too good for the client from what he said. So you'll just have to do your best won't you?' And off he went. It was getting on for opening time at the Devereux and he was conscientious about his duties to chambers in that direction.

Tam Pearse pulled off the red ribbon and opened out the papers before him, full of excitement and anticipation. An attempted murder did not come his way everyday by any means. In point of fact this was the first one that Tam had ever had. Tam first needed to know what was the case alleged against his new client, Yusuf Erim of Tiverton Street, Newington. At that time, he was told, there was considerable racial tension between Greek Cypriots living in London, in particular south of the Thames round about the Elephant and Castle area and their supposed compatriots, the Turkish Cypriots, who tended to congregate in North London round the area of Pentonville. His instructions showed that there had been quarrels between the two factions and in particular between his client and the man he was said to have attempted to murder, Andrea Papadopolous of Wardle Street, South Clapton. On Friday 3rd February last Yusuf Erim had been visiting his sister, Meral, who had bettered herself in life in the eyes of her family, by training and getting a job as a nurse at the Homerton Hospital in Clapton. Yusuf had been accompanied by his friend, Ismet Celic, who was very attracted to one Julietta Papadopolous, Meral's friend and a Greek Cypriot. For Ismet, as for Julietta, the barriers of different race created no problems; in spite of this, a true liking developed. In the case of Ismet, it was a good deal more than liking. Although normally sharing the dislike of all other Turks for Greeks, in the case of Julietta Papadopolous, he had fallen in love in a serious way. Like Shakespeare's Romeo for that other Juliet, it was a case of 'My only love sprung from my only hate'. Ismet was probably not very strong on Shakespeare, Tam reflected, as he read his papers, and may not even have been very much into Robert Burns, but when first he had met Julietta, he would probably have

31

met the case that Burns had had in mind when he wrote: 'But to see her was to love her, Love but her and love for ever'. However that may have been, he had jumped at the chance of seeing her in the company of her brother, since at that stage of things, according to her strict morality, that was the only way he could.

After leaving the Nurses' Hostel, close to the hospital in Clifden Road, it was necessary for the two young men to pass through Wardle Street on the way to Homerton Station and eventually the way home. Andrea Papadopolous lived in Wardle Street, and was fond of a drink of a Friday evening with his friends in the nearby Derby Arms. What is more he knew of, and strongly disliked, his sister's friendship for Ismet Celic, who he had seen earlier that night on his way towards Clifden Road with another Turkish Cypriot. This well-known pub was a favourite with the local Greek Cypriots. As well as all the obvious wares of a London public house, it served more exotic drinks to cater for its clientele, including a particularly cheap brand of Ouzo, that form of Schnapps made from aniseed and refined to a high concentration of alcohol, which is, and was such a favourite of the Greeks. Andrea had been drinking for a little time and was feeling happy, a feeling which went through a rapid change to anger when he spotted the two young Turkish Cypriots walking through his territory as if they owned it. Words were exchanged, blows were struck. A serious fight developed; the two Turks were heavily outnumbered and were getting much the worse of things outside the pub. Ismet managed to escape and, thinking that his friend would do the same, ran off in the direction of the station with not much harm done. But Yusuf was not so lucky and received a severe mauling, before the licensee of the Derby Arms ran out with two of his barmen and managed to break it up, hauling several Greeks from the unfortunate Yusuf and allowing him to escape, and then to run a twisting route to evade pursuit; eventually to find his way home, bruised, battered and vengeful. So Yusuf brooded. It was an insult to the whole of

32

Islam, but in particular, to Turkish Cypriots living in London. There were many of them, but he worried in particular for his sister, Meral, and about her friend, Julietta, who seemed to be so strongly attached to Ismet. Did Papadopolous know about Meral? Would he try to do her any harm? He must not be allowed to get away with it. He must be warned off. But how to do it? Yusuf knew that Papadopolous had a cousin Callimachus, who stayed near the Elephant in Brunton Street on his occasional visits to London from Cyprus, and he had heard that Andrea Papadopolous was working on a building site near Ludgate Circus, repairing the bomb damage still very much present in that area of London, for the building contractor, Murphy's. It would not be very difficult to get some further details because he knew another man who did the same. When he clocked in for work at the yard that Thursday morning, Papadopolous was given a message that very early that morning, there had been a call for him from his cousin to say that he had just arrived in London, but had to go straight out; could Andrea come round and see him for a drink and a meal that night, any time after eight o'clock? And so, that night, a week later on 10th February, found Yusuf Erim sitting in his battered Austin car in Duke's Yard on the way to the cousin's lodgings. Beside him in the car, but concealed from view, there was a highly illegal, sawn-off shotgun loaded with solid shot. At last, he saw a group of men approaching and recognised Papadopolous among them.

So, he had come with friends, which made it all a bit more difficult. But it was too late to turn back now. Yusuf Erim had wound down the window of his car and called out to Papadopolous. The Greek Cypriot was not afraid, even though he was in enemy territory. He had his friends with him and Erim seemed to be alone as he approached the open window and started to bow down his head for an exchange of insults. But, as he did so, Erim lifted the shotgun and pulled the trigger. Papadopolous fell to the ground and the car at once drove off. His friends gathered round the prostrate figure expecting it to be the corpse of their friend, Andrea, but surprisingly it moved. He had not been killed after all, and was not obviously bleeding. The shot must have gone over his head as he bent down, and in a fleeting second, saw the weapon being raised. He was, in any event, so shocked that he could not speak to his friends, but only gibber wordlessly at them.

And so it all came out. The men, and Papadopolous himself, would never have reported it to the police. Any more than Yusuf himself would have dreamed of reporting that he had been quite badly beaten up on his visit to Clapton. It was not the sort of thing they, or any of them, did. But some account had to be given to the nurse at Guy's Hospital when Papadopolous was left there by his friends, who had then slipped silently into the night without leaving their own names and addresses. The hospital called the police at once. Any violent crime had to be reported and this one seemed, at first, to be very serious. Papadopolous was put to bed, still silent. However the police were able to establish his identity from the contents of his pockets, and next day he had recovered his powers of speech. Notwithstanding the unwritten code, there seemed to be no escape for Andrea Papadopolous when the police came next day and took him down to Stoke Newington Police Station for questioning. He had to give some account of what had happened to him the night before and so, reluctantly he did so, but said that he had no idea as to who his attacker might have been.

The police had, of course, been called the night before to the scene of the crime by startled neighbours, but on arrival had found only a deserted Duke's Yard with no sign of any fracas, except for a small crowd of shocked locals. One of these however, George Tallack, a retired policeman himself, had been passing by at the time of the incident. He had seen the stationary car. He had noticed the window being lowered and a string of words in a foreign tongue being addressed to a small group of men passing through the Yard. One of these had gone over towards the car, leant forward, and then there had been a very loud bang and the man had fallen to he ground apparently dead, while the car drove off at speed. The man's friends had rushed up to him and helped him to his feet. Miraculously he had survived the brutal attack. His own offers of assistance had been brushed aside and the group of men had rushed away. His old training, however, had caused him to note the number of the car as it drove hurriedly away.

All of this was set out in the papers now before Tam but they gave little hint of what the defence would be. Of course it would be for the prosecution to prove their case to the jury beyond all reasonable doubt, or there could be no conviction. But on the evidence it did not look to Tam as if they would find that too difficult, should the defendant plead 'not guilty'. It must be his decision but it was for him to advise his client about it. A plea of 'guilty', saving the court's time, would be likely to be met with a more lenient sentence from the judge. Tam noticed, with interest, that there appeared to be no previous convictions recorded against Yusuf Erim; the police had confirmed as much. Unlike Andrea Papadopolous, who they very fairly conceded had quite a considerable 'previous history' which had included, Tam noticed with interest, several convictions for violence, including a serious one of 'causing grievous bodily harm with intent'. Perhaps on a plea of 'guilty', he might just be able to keep Yusuf Erim out of prison, in view of the extenuating circumstances of the previous beating up? But then he thought that that would be extremely unlikely, in view of the seriousness of the offence in question. It was after all attempted murder that was alleged, and with the use of a 12-bore shotgun at that, and in a densely populated part of London so that others might have seen it, as they had; and would also have had their lives put into danger.

A few afternoons later, Challen opened the door of Tam's room at 6, Damson Court and ushered in Mr Birley of Fearnley Davies, that well-known firm of Walworth solicitors for whom he had already had one or two outings with a reasonable success rate, and also the defendant Yusuf Erim. As they sat down in his room, Tam looked at Yusuf Erim with interest. Young, rather good-looking he thought, slim and no more than medium height, he was neatly dressed and was actually wearing a suit and tie. The case for the prosecution was clearly set out in the depositions, the careful transcript of the evidence which had been given in the Magistrates' Court when the defendant had been committed for trial at the Central Criminal Court of London, the Old Bailey. Mr Birley had attended on behalf of the defendant and, quite rightly and in accordance with well-established practice, had asked almost no questions. He had 'reserved the defence' for the later and all-important trial. This gave the prosecution no clues as to what the defence would be and, most importantly, no opportunity to make their own further enquiries, so as to be able to give evidence at the hearing to disprove any vital point it raised.

Introductions were completed. Tam Pearse noticed with relief that his client spoke very good English, with a touch of an accent the police were fond of describing as 'Mediterranean'. He seated his new client, and old and favourite solicitor client, in front of him with Mr Birley occupying his rather comfortable chair, and Yusuf Erim sitting rather nervously on a harder one. It reflected, he thought cynically, his own rather uncomfortable position as well as the difference in age between him and his solicitor. It would all be up to the defendant himself, should he agree to give evidence on his own behalf, and his witnesses, if any, and of course, to Tam as his counsel to get him out of this mess on the very first occasion that he had been in any trouble with the Law.

'So, what did happen that night, Mr Erim?' Tam asked politely.

'Well, Mr Pearse, it's just like they say at the early court and now set down 'ere, in these papers. I knew 'im, of course, and we'd had a few words in the past. But nothing serious,

36

you might say. But then, I went to visit me sister, with Ismet, the friend of 'er friend. As we was passing 'em, with no offence at all, 'e stuck out 'is leg 'n' tripped me up and they was onto me, all of 'em, about six or seven knockin' the daylights out 'o me. But 'e was the worst, Andrea. 'E was using a cosh 'e 'ad in 'is pocket. Even 'is pals told 'im to stop.'

'And you reported all this to the police?' Tam asked.

'No I didn't, but they got to 'ear about it later when all of this brew up.'

'All of what?'

'Well I couldn't let it pass, worse could have come of it from this man Papadopolous, 'e 'ad to be warned off, you call heem, shown 'e couldn't get away with it, or 'e might have done some 'arm to Meral.'

'So what did you do?'

'Well, I got a message to heem to come to see his cousin, and then I waited for heem where I knew 'e would pass, with the gun I got from a friend.'

'Did anyone have a licence for it?' Tan Pearse asked, knowing what the answer would be, but Mr Birley interjected respectfully:

'Nobody is charged with illegal possession of a firearm, Mr Pearse, only with attempted murder.'

'Well then, let's come to that Mr Erim, did you try to murder that man, that night?'

'Oh, no, Mr Pearse, that I never meant, not really to 'urt heem, only to scare heem, I can prove it.'

'How can you prove it?' Tam asked, reasonably enough he thought.

37

'That is for me to say? Is that not right, I get chance to say myself when they try me? Is not so? They 'ave commit me for trial at Old Bailey, then I can say.'

'It is certainly correct that you have been committed for trial for attempted murder, and that of course, if you wish you can give evidence on your own behalf at your own trial. But you really should let us know what your defence is, if you really have one. So we can advise you properly. It doesn't look too good you know. When you call the man over and he bends down and you fire this lethal weapon off at him at very short range. You could hardly have missed him, but somehow it seems that you did. So, if you can really prove that you had no intention of killing him, please tell me?'

'No, it is for me to say at the trial. I say it then.'

And he was quite adamant about it. No matter what Tam Pearse asked he would say no more. There was no question of a plea of guilty, either to attempted murder or to anything else. Tam carefully explained that he could have a quiet word with counsel for the prosecution, Mr Morton Tailor, who he knew quite well, he might be prepared to accept a plea to some lesser offence. Although Tam was not too hopeful, it might be possible, with the agreement of the judge who was to try the case, to persuade him to accept a plea to 'attempting to cause grievous bodily harm' and even, in view of the past history, he might escape going to prison at all. Tam was not too hopeful but he put the idea forward. It would save a lot of the court's time. There would only be a short morning of it. Ascot was on and he knew that Morton Tailor was mad on racing. But Yusuf was resolved. He would not plead 'guilty' to anything at all. No one had charged him with anything but attempted murder of Andrea Papadopolous, and he had not tried to murder that man. He would plead 'not guilty', he would give his own evidence and then he would give his proof.

Mr Birley argued with him gently but he would not be budged. Tam Pearse pointed out the difficulty. He had admitted that he had borrowed the 12-bore shotgun from some friend he had always resolutely refused to identify. It would mean that Tam would have to persuade the jury that a man who fired that weapon, at point blank range, at another man, had had no intention of killing him. In view of the weapon and the very short range, it was not going to be easy, particularly since Yusef had obviously had very good cause to wish him ill. As he himself was the very first to admit.

'I 'ad to do something, Mr.Pearse, 'e might have 'ad a go at Meral next, if I don' do notting,' he said logically enough, but doing his case no good. He still would give no clue as to his so-called proof that he had not attempted to kill his enemy. Tam just had to leave it unresolved and remained unhappy, since he liked to win his cases if he could and to persuade a reluctant client to enter the right plea and above all to understand him as well as he could. In this case, he certainly did not but after all, he consoled himself, it was for the client to make the vital decisions and up to him to do the best for him that he possibly could in difficult circumstances.

And so it was that, with not much hope or joyful expectancy, that Tam Pearse set off with his barrister's red bag of wig and gown upon his shoulders and his briefcase in his hand, down Fleet Street and in the direction of Ludgate Circus and then the Old Bailey, on a fine morning in June. When he had put on the finery and adjusted the angle of his wig to his satisfaction in the robing room mirror, he made his way down to Court Number One. The case was very honoured. It was, after all, an attempted murder and rated the most important court. There being no High Court Judge present that day, the case was to be presided over by His Honour Judge Beesleigh, the Recorder of London and the most senior judge on the roll of those always officiating at the Central Criminal Court, to give the Old Bailey its official title. Tam had a brief word with Mr Birley, his instructing solicitor, at the door of the court and discovered, with no surprise, that nothing had changed. Yusuf Erim still kept as silent as he always had as to his 'defence', if there really was one. Except, of course, that there is always the important point that it is for the prosecution to prove their case, if they can. Including the all-important question of the intent to do murder which the defendant must be shown to have, without any reasonable doubt, at the time in question.

Morton Tailor was already sitting in his place in court and looked up expectantly as Tam made his way into counsel's row. By tradition, prosecuting counsel sat closer to the judge than counsel for the defence did. Tam had found in the past that this sometimes produced an unexpected advantage for him. It meant that when he was standing up, and he was a big man, Tam himself, sitting beside him in counsel's row, would be screened from the critical gaze of the judge himself. There were just a few occasions when prosecuting counsel might be 'on his feet', when he happened to be addressing the jury, for instance, and about to make the one telling point for which the defence had no answer. The jury might be looking at him with rapt attention as he was just coming to that vital point. That would be the moment for their attention to be distracted, if it could be done. After all, all is fair in love and war, and a trial by jury is certainly war for the counsel taking part in it. Of course it would not do to be found out but how could one be? Sir Edward Marshal Hall, that great advocate of Victorian times, had had the trick of having a pile of law books beside him. When this crucial point was reached he would 'accidentally' give it a nudge so that the books fell with a loud bang and he would rise to his full considerable height, full of apologies and apparent contrition. By the time the ushers had collected up the books, the moment would have passed and the jury would be back to wondering what they were going to have for dinner that night. That trick was now too well-known, but Tam Pearse had found that if it just happened that he should, for instance, take off his wig and examine its lining with apparent irritation... then apparently snatch at an insect, crush it and throw it impatiently over his shoulder; why then it might be that when he looked up, every eye in the jury would be fixed upon him with the unspoken question being asked, 'That guy must have fleas in his wig? No, surely not? But what else can he be doing?' rather than listening to that very telling point that his opponent was just making.

'Good Morning, dear friend,' said Morton, although Tam had not realised that he was such a very dear friend. 'And what's it going to be? A plea of guilty as charged is what it looks like to me.'

'Certainly not, it's going to be "not guilty".'

He paused for a moment and looked visibly disconcerted; so Tam had been right in thinking that he might have wanted to slip away to Ascot for the Gold Cup that fine day.

'"Not guilty" to anything at all? You aren't going to ask me to take a plea to "attempting to commit grievous bodily harm"? I might consider that and have a word with the DPP?'

The DPP was the Director of Public Prosecutions, whose representative was sitting just behind Morton Tailor looking interested. Perhaps he too, had had aspirations for a short day in court that day.

'No, no the plea will be "not guilty", I am firmly instructed,' Tam said firmly.

Yusuf Erim was ushered into the dock, flanked by the usual warders to prevent any possible escape on his part, by leaping over the rails, possibly even to attack the judge. It did not look as if he would have any such thought in mind, Tam thought. He was looking very young and very respectable, wearing the same sober suit as he had had on when visiting him in the conference in Damson Court, with a clean shirt and sober tie. The very fact that he had been able to visit Tam, rather than for Tam to have to visit him in Wandsworth

41

Prison, was a recognition of his present clean record. Otherwise, for such a serious offence as attempted murder, he would never have been granted bail. Then the court usher gave the traditional call, 'All rise', and everyone got to their feet as Eustace Beesleigh, Recorder of London, made his entrance, up-staging everyone else, as was intended.

There followed the usual formalities of any criminal trial. The jurors-in-waiting were called into court. Twelve of them were ushered into the jury box and sworn in to 'duly try the several issues joined between Her Majesty, the Queen, and the prisoner at the bar, and true verdict make, according to the evidence'. They appeared to be a reasonable selection of Londoners, nine men and three women. At that time in the early 1960s, they all had to be householders. Perhaps they might have been likely to be just a little more responsible and better educated than the situation today, when anyone on the electoral roll under the age of 70 is liable to be summoned for jury service.

The Clerk of the Court rose to his feet and intoned:

'Yusuf Erim, you are charged on indictment that on the night of Friday, 10th February, in the year of Our Lord, 1960, at Duke's Yard, London, E9, you did attempt to murder Andrea Papadopolous. How say you? Are you "guilty" or "not guilty"?'

'Not guilty.' Yusuf spoke quietly and firmly, with a sort of quiet conviction that was impressive. Almost in spite of himself Tam began to wonder if, in spite of all appearances, he might even be able to pull some unexpected trick that would get him off this particularly vicious-looking hook.

Morton Tailor rose to his full height and began his opening to the jury. He recited the facts very much as they had appeared in Tam's own brief. He would call the injured man, and his sister, to prove the presence of the defendant at the earlier incident. Here there was a departure from the truth, as it had been presented to Tam, for the whole of the earlier incident was very much played down – just a question of a fight breaking out between two groups of young men of similar origin, but widely different race and religion, with no particular blame attached to Papadopolous, although it was conceded that the defendant might have suffered some injuries on that earlier occasion.

'Just the sort of injuries that would be likely to make him bear a grudge against the man he later attempted to murder, you may think, members of the jury,' said Morton Tailor, pausing for dramatic effect and gesturing towards Yusuf Erim, who was looking quietly unconcerned, a faintly contemptuous expression on his face.

And then he came to the day in question, Friday, 3rd February, when Papadopolous had received a message at work. It would be produced in evidence. It said, and the jury could read it themselves, that his cousin Callimachus, was visiting London and staying in Brunton Street near the Elephant and Castle, very much the home territory of Yusuf Erim, he emphasised with a knowing look. The note asked Papadopolous to meet him that evening for a drink and to call for him first. It was all quite untrue. Callimachus was not in London at that time. The telephone message received by Murphy's was a fake. The prosecution could not prove that it was the defendant who had sent it or caused it to be sent. The foreman at the building site could only say that the caller had had a foreign accent and that applied to almost everyone connected with the case.

'But, in view of what was to happen so soon afterwards, members of the jury, you may have little difficulty in coming to the conclusion that this was a deliberate trap set by the defendant, or by his friends at his instigation, to lure Papadopolous out of the safety of his own home area down into South London, the home territory of the defendant. For what was to happen as Papadopolous was making his way with some of his friends, quietly and peacefully through Duke's Yard on his way to his cousin's house, where it would be known that he must pass, but there was a car, which belonged to the defendant, and with him inside it. He lowered the window as the group of young men passed by, called out to Papadopolous by name, and when he went over and bent down to the open car window, what did he do? He raised a shotgun, which he had hidden beside him in the car, and fired it at once at point blank range. It is a miracle that he missed. But the prosecution say that there could be no clearer evidence of an attempt to murder than that act. Although it missed, it left the victim so badly injured that he could not speak and had to be taken by his friends to the nearby Guy's Hospital, where mercifully he recovered next day. He was not, at first, inclined to name his attacker but happily a witness, one George Tallack, himself a retired member of the Metropolitan Police Force, had been passing by at the time of the incident in question. He had been too late to intervene in any way, but had noted down the number of the car that he had seen speed off. That number was traced and the car was found to be registered in the name of the defendant, who now admits to having been present that night. Indeed…' Morton Tailor paused and looked hard at Tam as if daring him to challenge it…'I understand he even admits to having fired the shot.'

Tam said nothing. Indeed, there was nothing that he could say since this was exactly what Yusuf had admitted to. Morton Tailor's thought 'So, why on earth does he not plead guilty so that we can all be done with it?' was all too obvious, Tam had to concede, but only silently and to himself. And so, the case for the prosecution unfolded. First there was PC Noakes, who was one of the first two officers to arrive in Duke's Yard in response to a telephone call from a frightened resident, who had heard a shot fired and the sound of running feet, and rushed to look out of his window to see men running and a departing car speeding off. There was George Tallack, ex-PC, to give his account of events, which was not much to the point since he had arrived only in time to see the car stationary and a man talking at the window of it before the

44

shot was fired, and he could provide no real ideas as to what had caused it all, but only the important fact that the shot had been fired and from that car and at very close range. Of course, he had taken down the number of the car as it shot past him out of Duke's Yard and away into the darkness of that February evening; and he had handed it to the police when they arrived at the scene. He was duly commended by the judge for having done so and departed with a smile of satisfaction; old training had paid off for his day out of retirement and back in the firing-line for a brief moment.

Then there was Staff Nurse Earnshaw of Guy's Hospital, who gave evidence of the admission of Andrea Papadopolous to her ward. A careful examination revealed that he had suffered no visible, physical injury, but at first he stayed silent; apparently because he simply was unable to answer the necessary questions she put to him. The friends who had brought him into the hospital had all slipped off as soon as they had deposited him in the waiting room in casualty, without leaving their own names and addresses, or indeed those of the injured man, saying only that their friend had been shot. However, she had looked at the few possessions taken from his pockets when he was put into hospital pyjamas, and had found the telephone number of a relative, his sister Julietta, and had managed to reach her, as she herself was a nurse at Homerton Hospital. The patient's identity was established and she had informed the police at once, as hospital regulations required that she should. Julietta was called as a witness, briefly, to fill in any gap there might have been as to her brother's identity. Tam noticed that she seemed ill at ease in her brief appearance, and kept glancing at a good-looking young man sitting in the middle of the court, who Mr Birley identified to Tam as Ismet Celic, who had played such a central role in the whole history of the case, but who neither side was destined to call as a witness. Clearly Julietta had divided loyalties in the matter and Tam decided that only harm might come if he were to ask her any awkward questions about her relationship with either her brother or with Ismet Celic.

And then there was Andrea Papadopolous. He looked a young thug, and that was good for Tam's purposes. But, at least he had had a job at the time. He gave his evidence with a defiant air and Tam glanced down at the list of previous convictions that the police had supplied him with. They had had to, of course. The criminal law was weighted to give a fair deal to any defendant who appeared in any criminal court. It all dated from the days before 1907 when defendants were allowed to give evidence on their own behalf for the first time. Before then they were not, and the rules had been framed with that in mind. The rules remained, although, of course defendants have been able to give evidence in support of their own case for very many years now. A defendant's 'previous convictions' would be known to the court and to the prosecution, but not to the jury, the judges of fact in any case and the traditional bastions of liberty for the individual against possible oppression by the police.

It was thought that the knowledge of what the defendant had done before, perhaps exactly that offence for which he was charged and brought before them, would be too much for them to try the new matter fairly. So, they were not, and are not, told about it. Unless that is, the defendant 'puts his character in issue' by launching an attack on the character of one of the prosecution witnesses. Fairness then requires that the defendant's own previous bad character should be made known. Of course the same applies should any defendant with a string of previous convictions be silly enough to suggest when giving evidence, that he was a man of good character. That would be too much and the jury would soon be undeceived, because the police could then reveal the true state of things. The list of convictions provided for Papadopolous showed, Tam was pleased to note, several for violence. Yusuf Erim was a man of good character so that he should be able to make some reasonable use of this in cross-

46

examination without fear of any riposte by Morton Tailor, who could only sit silently beside him listening to the thoroughly bad character of his principal witness, knowing that the defendant himself had a perfectly good record, and was immune from any similar attack by the prosecution.

Andrea Papadopolous gave his evidence well enough, although Tam thought that he looked decidedly uneasy when describing the events of the earlier incident on 3rd February. The vital occasion in question on February 10th, when he had been shot at and injured, he was firm about.

'I never done nothing to 'im, nor even said a word. We was just passing by and saw 'im on the way. Never thought of 'im at all when I got the message. We was going to see Callimachus for a drink, 'e 'ad phoned. Or I thought 'e 'ad. To suggest it. Then we saw 'im,' he gestured derisively at the defendant sitting impassively in the dock, ''e called me over. So I went and bent down to the window, when there was this great bang and I 'eard no more till I was in 'ospital.'

So Tam rose to his feet to do his best with some rather unpromising material, he thought. Still, there were some good points to be made.

'You come from the Greek part of Nicosia in Cyprus, don't you?'

'Yes, I do.'

'And the defendant is a Turkish-Cypriot, coming originally from Famagusta?'

'I don't know where 'e comes from, but 'e's Turkish-Cypriot, all right.'

'And the Greeks don't much like the Turks in Cyprus, do they? Or for that matter nor do the Greek-Cypriots living in London like the Turkish-Cypriots living here either?'

'Not always.'

'Not ever?'

'Maybe not.'

'And, in particular, is it right that you specially disliked one of them, a young man called Ismet Celic, who had become a very good friend of your sister, Julietta?'

'No, it not right that that man should go out with Julietta, 'e is not even a Christian let alone Greek Orthodox.'

'And had you seen him, Ismet Celic, that night of the first incident, Friday 3rd February, when it was the Turks who were injured outside the Derby Arms in your home area?'

'Yes, I see 'im passing through, off to see Julietta with that man,' and he gestured towards Yusuf Erim sitting quietly in the dock.

'So, it was no coincidence, the fight that night? You and your friends had been laying in wait for him? Anxious to see him off and make an example of him...? And the defendant just happened to be there, so he got beaten up as well, but rather worse, was that it?'

'I mean that man no 'arm, but 'e was in the fight too, yes.'

'And there were six of you and only two of them?'

'Maybe.'

He said this reluctantly; but the point was made, for what it was worth. Tam Pearse might have got some of the jury's sympathy, but perhaps that would not count for very much, when it was at the expense of providing a clear reason for revenge and, the prosecution were sure to say, the reason for the attempted murder with which they had charged the defendant.

'And when you saw him on 10th February, he was on his own, sitting in his car and, once more you were with friends.

Did you think of resuming the fight and attacking him once more?'

'No, we was just going out to 'ave a drink with Cally, when 'e call me. I just went over to speak to 'im and then there was a great "bang", and everything went black until I wake up in the 'ospital bed.'

'But, of course, you are no stranger to violence are you, Mr Papadopolous?' Tam Pearse asked courteously. 'Were you not convicted of causing grievous bodily harm with intent upon one John Palmer at this very court, on 21st August, 1958 when you were sentenced to 12 months' imprisonment?'

The witness said nothing but looked sullen and nasty and dangerous...

'...It is not all that long since you would have been released from serving that sentence. And that wasn't the only one for crimes of violence, was it?'

But the witness remained silent with the same sullen expression on his face.

'...not your only conviction for violent crime by a very long way?'

Tam had the official list of his convictions before him and there was no way that they could be denied. That last sentence had followed quickly upon others spaced out over the past seven years and starting with common assault, and following soon after a period of Borstal training for an indecent assault upon a young girl of 16 years of age. Tam dwelt on every detail and watched Morton Tailor squirming in discomfort out of the corner of his eye. It was all very satisfactory when he knew very well that there could be no possible come back upon Yusuf, in view of his own unblemished record.

A point Tam soon made very clear when the last prosecution witness was called.

This was Detective Inspector George Fothergill, the officer in charge of the case and the last prosecution witness. The most experienced man they had, of course, left to create a last good impression on the jury. To put right, if possible, perhaps the decidedly bad impression that Tam thought that Papadopolous himself must have made on the jury. His evidence-in-chief was factual and formal, filling a few gaps left by the evidence of others, but not adding a lot to it. As the arresting officer, he had formally charged the defendant. And cautioned him that he need say nothing in answer to the charge made against him, but that anything he did say would be taken down in writing, and might be used in evidence against him at his trial. He agreed with Tam at once that Yusuf Erim had been perfectly co-operative with the police in every way. He agreed that he was a man of excellent previous good character. Not only had he been in continuous employment as a warehouseman since he had come to England three years before, but his employers spoke highly of him. Tam had, of course, established all of this beforehand through the excellent Mr Birley, since he did not want to run the risk of getting the wrong answer to any such important questions. The detective inspector also agreed with him immediately that the defendant was perfectly justified in giving no explanation as to what had happened, or how it had happened, that night. That was his right and the inspector was fair-minded enough to say so. And then Tam asked a last question. For no particular reason, although later events showed that it was what Bridge players call something in the nature of a 'psychic bid'.

'Tell me, Inspector, did you, or any other police officer so far as you know, ever go back to Duke's Yard that night, or for that matter on any other occasion, to make any kind of physical examination of it or of its condition?'

'Well no, sir, I didn't see any call for that, there was no need.'

So then it was Tam's turn to open the case for the defence. Had he been calling witnesses, it would have been his right to open his case with a speech to the jury. But he had no witnesses to call except the defendant himself. No other friend of his had been there and it might not have helped very much if anyone had been.

'M'Lud, I call Yusuf Erim,' Tam said with more assurance than he felt, and Yusuf was duly escorted to the witness box, where being a Muslim, he duly swore upon the Koran that the evidence he was about to give would be the truth, the whole truth and nothing but the truth.

Tam took him quickly through the events of 3rd February, and the beating up that he and Ismet Celic had received at the hands of the Greeks in Clapton, and then asked with some trepidation:

'So, what did you think was going to happen after that night, Mr Erim, when you were beaten up?'

'Well. I think I 'ave to do something. They must 'ave known that we were going to see my sister an' 'er friend Julietta. Of course we knew well enough that 'er brother, Andrea, no like for Ismet to like Julietta. 'E must have been waiting for us with 'is friends and 'e did us up proper. I 'ad a black eye and my ribs were 'urt quite bad. So, I think that they must be warned it is not so easy to 'urt the Turks; or per'aps they do some 'arm to Meral. They must be warned off. So when I 'ear that Andrea is coming to see 'is cousin then, yes, I did wait for heem in Duke's Yard.'

'With a shotgun?' Tam prompted nervously.

He knew there was no getting away from the fact that Yusef Erim had had one. It had belonged to a friend he would not identify, and a nasty-looking piece of work it was. Exhibit 1 in the case, it was lying on the table in the centre of the

51

court for all to see, and Tam wished it had not been. It had been roughly sawn-off so that it was easier to use at close quarters, and that meant that it was intended not for the legitimate purpose of shooting game of some sort, but for the far from legitimate purpose of use for some sort of crime. In fact, for shooting at, or at least for threatening, human rather than animal game.

'Yes, but it was not loaded.'

'But it went off?'

'Yes, 'e went off but not with a live bullet... I loaded heem with a blank. You call it, without the bullets... a blank cartridge.'

So there it was. This was the secret defence that Yusuf had been keeping up his sleeve, even from his own defence team. Whatever else it might have been, and Tam Pearse could think of several offences of a minor character that would have fitted quite well, but at least no one could say that there could have been any attempt to murder, or even to do any serious bodily harm to anyone, if it had only been a blank cartridge. But would it stand up? Tam glanced at Morton Tailor to see how he would take the news, in time to see him in earnest conversation with the solicitor from the Department of Public Prosecutions, sitting on the benches in the well of the court immediately in front of him.

'So you did not have any intention of harming Andrea Papadopolous that night?'

'No, I no wish to hurt heem... only to scare... to scare heem off.'

Well that was it, and not at all bad Tam thought as he resumed his seat and Morton Tailor rose up to begin his cross-examination. As he did so, Tam noticed that his solicitor was whispering to Inspector Fothergill, who hurried out of court at once.

'So it was all quite deliberate, was it? The false message to get Andrea Papadopolous to come down into your own area? Where you knew he was likely to be, so that you could lie in wait for him in ambush?'

'Yes, sir, that all true... you see, he 'ad to be taught a lesson, 'e would not 'ave stopped without 'e do some 'arm to me or worse, to my Meral... 'e 'ad to be shown that 'e could not go on like that.'

'So, you had in your possession that awful weapon...?' said Morton, looking at Exhibit 1, 'just to frighten him.'

Disbelief was in every inflection of the cultured voice.

'That shotgun could maim or disable, or most likely, at close quarters, it would be likely to kill, would it not?'

'Yes 'e could, but not when there was only a blank cartridge in heem.'

'But you wanted him out of the way, after what he had done to you, and he partly admits it, you thought you had every reason to make sure that he did not do it again to you? Or for that matter, to your sister, Meral? That was the reason that you were lying in wait for him. The real truth is that you intended to murder him, as the indictment charges against you... that is the real truth, isn't it?'

But Yusuf would have none of it. With righteous indignation he repeated, 'I want to scare the daylights out of heem yes, 'e deserve that for what 'e done and what 'e might 'ave done. But not to keel heem, if so I would 'ave used real bullets and that I did not do.'

At that moment Inspector Fothergill came hurrying back into court and caught hold of prosecuting counsel's gown to give it a sharp tug, as he stood on his feet cross-examining the defendant.

'My Lord, will your Lordship kindly excuse me for a moment while I take instructions,' said Morton Tailor to the judge; and he and Fothergill whispered something, giving him every appearance of satisfaction.

'Mr Erim, I have just been informed that it is quite impossible to buy any blank cartridges for a 12-bore shotgun, they simply are not manufactured; what you have just been telling My Lord and the members of the jury must be a pack of lies.'

'No, I tell no lies. Mebbe you cannot buy 'em but I make 'em. I take a live cartridge. Then I take out the cardboard at the end of heem. I pour out all the shots. There was a pile of them. Then I put back in some cotton wool to fill the gap. Then I put heem in the shotgun. When I call that man over to me, I pull the trigger and the gun goes off, but nothing never hits heem 'cos there's nothin' there anyway to 'it 'im with.'

Yusuf Erim looked quietly satisfied and continued:

'I only want to scare 'im, you see 'e deserve to be scared.'

And nothing that Morton could do or say would shake him from that.

And that was the end of the evidence. Tam thought that young Yusuf had done very well and he did not feel inclined to tempt fate by asking any clever, last minute question in re-examination, which might only have the effect of undoing all the good work already done.

Since Tam called no other witness, it gave him the right to address the jury last. So, Morton Tailor spoke first and went through all the evidence, with all the care that he always did. Without that piece of evidence, very awkward for the prosecution, that the 12-bore cartridge had been a blank, it would have been an open and shut case. In spite of Yusuf's good previous character and Papadopolous's previous string of convictions and provocative behaviour. But then he came to that rather awkward difficulty about it all that Tam had foreseen.

'Now, members of the jury, we come to his surprising piece of evidence that all the time, having lured his opponent down into his part of London, where his friends, the Turkish-Cypriots, dwelt in large numbers and where the Greek-Cypriots were notably scarce, and having armed himself with a lethal weapon, which you see before you on the table, Exhibit 1, he would have you believe that he had first taken out all the shot from the cartridge that he was going to use. How would he have known how to do that? This simple man who had had to borrow the weapon in the first place.'

Well, that was the bit that Tam did not much like himself, so he resorted to his own well-tried tactic. Not, like Sir Edward Marshall Hall of the past, to push over a pile of books to distract the jury. It could have done so only for a few moments anyway. Tam Pearse's own method was a little more subtle. He took off his wig just as Morton Tailor was saying, '...he would have you believe'. It was rather a hot day and he noticed the eyes of two or three of the jury turn towards him. What was this chap doing, being improperly dressed on such a solemn occasion? they seemed to be thinking. But he was now looking intently into the wig held in his hand. After a few moments, his hand dived inside it and he snatched at the lining, then lifted his hand and stared at his forefinger and thumb which were clenched together, before turning and making a flicking motion over his shoulder. He turned back to make another search of the inside of his wig, then shook it, made another pounce and examined the result of that. He glanced up to be sure that Morton Tailor stood well between him and the hunched figure of Eustace Beesleigh on the Bench, but all was well and the only people paying attention to him were the jury. By this time he saw, with satisfaction, that every eye on the jury was fixed intently upon him. 'That man, in all his fancy clothes, has got nits in his wig' was clearly the thought in every mind.

'How could this man, this simple peaceful fellow, he would have you believe, have dared to tamper with a live, 12-bore cartridge?'

Morton Tailor looked at the jury with a puzzled but sceptical expression on his aesthetic face. But the attention of the jury was lost to him as Tam made another pounce and flicked another non-existent insect over his shoulder, before putting his wig carefully back in its proper place and turning to face the jury with, he hoped, a bland and innocent expression. Morton Tailor had finished all he had to say and sat down.

And then it was Tam's turn to make what he could of a case which had at first seemed near hopeless but which now was full of possibilities for a glorious acquittal.

'May it please you, M'Lud,' he began with the time-honoured phrase.... 'Members of the jury, My Lord will tell you when he comes to his summing, that it is for the prosecution to prove their case, as it is in every other criminal case in this country, and you must find that it is proved to your satisfaction. That is to say, that it is not for the defendant to prove that he is innocent but for the prosecution to prove that he is guilty. That means that if you have any reasonable doubt about the matter at all, then the only verdict which you can properly return is a verdict of "not guilty".' It was worthwhile for Tam to labour the point since he was not, in fact, at all sure that Eustace Beesleigh would put the burden of proof quite as clearly as he had himself expressed it. Eustace was well known for his preference for the prosecution in any case. A preference said to relate to his own long experience while a member of the Bar before his elevation to the Bench, when he had himself been one of the prosecuting team at the Old Bailey, where he now sat dispensing justice. He might have been inclined to include the obligatory direction as to the onus of proof, as an aside in tones just above a whisper, so that it reached the ears of the court shorthand writer, sitting just below him, but might not reach the jury, or at least those hard of hearing sitting a little further off. In this way it would all be recorded and be upon the Court Record for all to see. No one could criticise him for not giving the obligatory warning to the jury, should the case go to the Court of Appeal. But the true course of justice, which was in the eyes of Eustace Beesleigh, a conviction in almost every case, would be achieved. So that it was better for Tam to make sure, when he knew that no one could possibly criticise him for making a correct statement of the law which might otherwise escape audible mention altogether, and so be sure that the jury had the point well in mind.

'In order to convict him of the very serious offence of attempted murder you would have to be sure, not that his own defence that the shot he fired was with a blank cartridge, but that you are convinced that it could not have been.'

Tam had asked the hard-working Mr Birley of Fearnley Davies and Co, his instructing solicitors, if he could possibly see that Julietta remained in court after she had given her evidence. This was easy enough to achieve since no witness may be released without the consent of the court and this would not be given without the agreement of the Defence. And there she sat, dark-haired, as one might expect a young Greek woman to be. With a lovely, pale complexion and, surely strangely for someone from Nicosia, startlingly blue eyes. She was joined, as Tam glanced at her, by another young man of Mediterranean aspect who sat down next to her. Tam had never seen Ismet Celic, since he had not been called as a witness for either side, but from the way that they looked at each other and his immediate taking of her hand, it seemed a reasonable guess that this was that same 'star-crossed lover' that Shakespeare had cast for that other Juliet.

'Members of the jury...' Tam continued, dragging his eyes away from the scene behind him, '...it may well be that you believe what my client has told you. Did he not appear to be the epitome of an honest witness? Remember that he is a young man of excellent previous character. Unlike his accuser, Andrea Papadopolous, who we all know is a man of very bad character and known violent disposition. Even if you are left in the slightest doubt about his innocence of any desire to hurt Papadopolous that night, how can you possibly be sure that his intention was to kill this other young man? Because that is what you would have to be sure of in order to find that the offence alleged against him was true and to return a verdict of "guilty of attempted murder". His account of the preparation of the 12-bore cartridge and the removal of the shot from it, and the substitution of cotton wool, has the ring of truth about it, does it not? Surely, at least it could be true? No one could be sure.

'It has certainly not been *disproved* by the prosecution in this case. It is for you to say, but remember, that you as a jury, like any other jury in a criminal case in this country, are the only judges of truth.'

Again, Tam thought that it would do no harm to remind the jury of this, in case they had been just a little bit swayed by Morton Tailor's impressive manner and apparent conviction of the strength of the case for the prosecution. Or in case they might be swayed by any views on the matter that might be inferred from the summing-up they would shortly be listening to from the lips of Eustace Beesleigh.

'You have heard, no doubt with horror, of the feuding and the fighting that is going on in London between those of Greek-Cypriot origin on the one hand, and those like my client, of Turkish-Cypriot origin on the other. We know that there is no such awful animosity between Julietta Papadopolous and the defendant's friend, Ismet Celic. There they sit.'

Tam paused to turn round and point out Julietta, that recent witness called for the prosecution, sitting next to the good-looking young Turk the jury had heard had been involved in the beating-up which had taken place on Friday,

58

3rd February. As the eyes of the jury turned upon them, they were looking into each other's eyes, oblivious to everything else. 'Members of the jury, might it be that some good could come out of this trial? A contest, you may think, not only between the prosecution with all the resources at its disposal, and the defendant standing there alone, but also a trial between the London Greek-Cypriots on the one hand and the London Turkish-Cypriots on the other?

'Might not a well-merited verdict by you of "not guilty" heal some wounds, build up some bridges, between these opposing forces of potential disorder?'

As Tam Pearse resumed his seat there was no ripple of applause. There never can be, in the fraught atmosphere of the Old Bailey when serious crime is at issue. But he felt a pleasing relaxation of tension in the air. He knew that he had been guilty of using what histrionics he could. But in a Trial-by-Jury, it was the jury that counted. Not for them the hard logic of the Law. The battle between the effect of one previously decided case against that of another; or at least, not only hard logic. They did not leave their own knowledge of human nature behind when they went into the jury box. Nor their hearts as well as their minds, Tam reflected. He also saw that he was not the only one to glance again at those two young figures behind him. Quite clearly as far as they were concerned, there was no bridge that needed to be re-built.

And then Eustace Beesleigh began his summing-up to the jury. For once he put it all on the line without apparent bias in favour of either party. As he always should, but all too rarely did. Then the jury filed out of court to consider their verdict. Mr Birley and Tam retired to the coffee room to revive themselves after the labours of the past couple of days. But they had hardly started on their second cups when everyone was summoned back to court with the news that the jury were agreed upon a verdict. This was a sure indication that there had been little in the way of dispute or disagreement between them, but which way? After everyone had resumed their seats, the jury came back in and Tam was pleased to note that every pair of eyes seemed to turn and look towards the solitary figure in the dock, flanked by his attendant prison warders. Eustace Beesleigh, Recorder of London, came back into court and took his seat as everyone respectfully stood up.

Then the Clerk of the Court rose to his feet to say:

'Will the foreman of the jury please stand up? Members of the jury, are you agreed upon your verdict?'

'We are agreed.'

'And how say you… is the defendant "guilty" or "not guilty" as charged in the indictment?'

'Not guilty, My Lord.'

'And that is the verdict of you all?'

'My Lord, it is.'

'Let the defendant be discharged,' said Eustace Beesleigh and Yusuf stepped out of the dock with a happy smile upon his face.

The jury had done their duty and were discharged for that day, to return on the next to complete their service. Mr Birley and Tam Pearse went outside the court to be surrounded by a throng of eager, enthusiastic Turkish-Cypriots who were the friends and relations of Yusuf, and then they soon went off. Morton Tailor came by and gave Tam a congratulatory smile. Members of the Bar never shake hands with each other. It is assumed that, being 'brothers in the law', everyone knows everyone else, so that it is considered rather bad form to do so.

'Well that is one that got away,' he said wryly.

'And quite right too,' Tam rejoined.

'Well, perhaps,' Morton Tailor replied. 'Maybe we did not do our homework properly.'

As a final word of parting on the subject, Tam reminded him, 'The truth will out.'

But he was ungracious enough to respond, 'But I wonder if it did?'

Well, Tam did have some last, lingering doubts himself, so he asked Mr Birley if he had time to drive them both through Duke's Yard on their way back.

Mr Birley knew it well, and had no difficulty in parking his car in roughly the same spot that Yusuf had parked his that fateful night of several months before. They looked across at a blank wall of some Mews garages on the other side of the yard.

'Well, that looks clean enough,' said Mr Birley. 'Surely if there had of been a loaded 12-bore cartridge fired at it from this range, which somehow missed Papadopolous, there would have been some very obvious marks to show for it?'

Tam made no reply and allowed him to keep his illusions. But was left wondering himself. Had he detected an area of some 18 inches square where there were the faint marks which might have been left by a spray of pellets, now blurred by several months of winter rains and summer sun? He could not be sure. Perhaps; anyway they could have been caused in any of a hundred other ways. Perhaps his eyes were deceiving him. Surely the police would have come to look, just as he and Mr Birley had just done? Perhaps they had and like Mr Birley, had seen nothing out of the ordinary. Or perhaps, knowing nothing of the evidence that Yusuf would give at his trial, they merely had not done their homework very well?

The Verbal

'What is Truth?'

...said Jesting Pilate

Of course we all rely on our police as the upholders of the law, as our protection from all those villains who wish to break it by assaulting us, by trying to break into our homes or rape our wives or daughters. They are a really wonderful body of men. Well certainly most of them are. Inevitably there is the occasional bent cop because after all, they are humans and subject to the same pressures as everyone else. However, they do want to be successful, they think that their prospects of promotion depend upon their success and of course, to a large extent, they must be right. But this does mean that once they have decided who has committed the crime and gone on to arrest him or her... well then, human nature comes into play, so not only do they want to be proved right, but occasionally the pressure to find evidence to convict the one they know to be guilty proves too much and an unscrupulous policeman will decide to improve his case by dishonest means.

Tam Pearse, a young barrister, started his career by doing criminal cases. They were then, as they are now, among the worst paid of all the work a barrister can get.

Probably for that reason they were in fairly good supply. English Law is founded on justice and it must be unjust to deny the suspected criminal the right to be defended by counsel just as able as the one who is going to conduct the case for the prosecution. So there was the 'dock brief' which meant that the accused who asked for one, in open court at the start of the sessions in question, was certain to be granted the right to be defended by some eager young barrister who was waiting in court, anxious to test out his skills, perhaps in a very serious case, and all for a very modest fee. This, in Tam's first days at the Bar, was only the derisory sum of £1-3s-6d. That meant little to Tam. It was a chance to get started, to begin the road to fame and fortune, to become a second Sir Edward Marshal Hall, the great defending barrister of Victorian times. And it had worked, or it was working. He had had some good successes in his earliest days. Solicitors sitting in court, waiting for their cases to come on, had listened, had noted his successes and even his valiant attempts for clients which had made all in court to be a little doubtful, but which had not quite succeeded in securing an acquittal. Now he had been noticed and had started to get some cases of his own, sent in to his clerk, Challen, an impressive figure for a barrister's clerk since he was also no less than the mayor of an important south coast town.

Tam Pearse had also come across the very occasional case of the bent cop, as he remembered as he now came hurrying in to his chambers in Damson Court, The Temple. He came up the stairs and into the clerk's room where Challen held court, surrounded by Maisie, the typist and maid of all work, and Peter the junior clerk to be greeted by Challen:

'Mr Pearse, you know you have a conference with James Hawkins of Purvis and Jarrold starting in a few minutes. Mr Hawkins has just 'phoned to say he and his client will be delayed for a short time, and I've just heard from the Bailey that the list has collapsed a bit and so your case of Regina versus Johnson could come on for hearing very soon... they also wanted to have confirmation of what they'd been told... that it *is* going to be a fight?'

'Well that is what the instructions say but it is not going to be easy,' said Tam, and he went on into his own room where his young pupil, Patsy Hornby, was already sitting at her desk. 'Good morning, Patsy, we are just going to have a conference in the latest Purvis and Jarrold brief. Have you had a look at it?'

Patsy Hornby looked up to say: 'Well, as a matter of fact, I have. Fascinating, but it looks open and shut to me. There seems to be no doubt that the Camden branch of Barclays Bank was receiving a delivery of cash on the morning in question. No doubt that a car drew up and four men wearing stocking masks jumped out and attacked the Securicor delivery men, wielding chair legs as truncheons and carrying off several bags of cash. No doubt the car that had been used was found later that day, quite empty of money bags, but with one chair leg carelessly dropped on the floor. No doubt that fingerprints were found upon it and no doubt that they belonged to our client, Bernie Johnson, very careless of him it must have been, particularly when he has a record as long as your arm... So why don't we just get him to plead guilty and try to get him a light sentence?'

'What *with his record*?' Tam was surprised at the very idea of a light sentence for Bernie Johnson. 'Anyway, he apparently says he is not guilty, that he wasn't anywhere near, but was somewhere quite different, so we have to do the best we can. No way he will plead guilty. I got him off once before and he thinks I can work miracles... but this time, a miracle it would have to be.'

Patsy was still very new at the criminal Bar. 'How can you possibly defend a man you know is guilty?'

'But I do not *know* that he is. What I may happen to think is quite another matter because it is not for me to decide. That is a matter for the great British jury. If he *told* me that he was guilty then the rules of our profession say quite clearly that I can only make a plea in mitigation of sentence for him, since that would mean that I was *knowingly* putting forward a false case. He is unlikely to do that, I think, but we shall soon see. Perhaps he has a foolproof alibi for the time in question. But I do have to admit that things look black for him... except for one thing...'

'Which is?'

'Well, the police do have some bad habits. When they know that they've got the right man then they want to be sure that he is convicted, which is all very right and proper. But sometimes they use the wrong means to try to make a conviction certain. "Planting" incriminating evidence at the time of arrest is one example. The "Verbal" is another. It consists of making a careful "note" of an incriminating statement, said to have been made by the defendant, often at the time of his arrest or when he is charged with the offence in question. In fact, the officer in question puts words into the defendant's mouth. The best example is almost farcical: "It's a fair cop, guv". Almost unbelievably, this unlikely admission is still sometimes attributed to a defendant who, in fact, has said nothing at all. It was so back in the days when I was a pupil. Of course, there are many cleverer and more believable examples than that but because of the prevalence of the untrue verbal arose the need for the rule that the accused should be "cautioned" by the arresting officer at the time of the arrest, and when the formal charge is put to him. "You are not obliged to say anything, but anything you do say, will be taken down in writing and may be given in evidence".'

Patsy looked horrified at what she had heard as she said, 'And you think they've done that here?'

'It certainly looks like it to me... not one, but two police witnesses, are going to say that when they eventually came across our client, some weeks later, they were in a police car near Hoxton market and just saw him. They say that they wound down the window of their car and called him over, and that he leant down and said, with no prompting at all, "If it's the blagging in the f***g High Street you mean... I don't mind going down for the motor, but I never rolled the geezer". And their two accounts are word for word the same. And they are meant to make up their notebooks completely independently of each other!'

There was a tap at the door which opened to admit Challen, who ushered in James Hawkins and Bernie Johnson, a sly-looking, smartly dressed young man, furtively looking about him as if to determine the possible means of escape.

Tam Pearse said, 'Please come in and take a seat...' which his visitors gratefully did. '...Now, Bernie things don't look too good for you. You will have seen the prosecution's case. It is all too clearly outlined in the depositions that were taken before the committing magistrates. They obviously thought that a case had been made out against you or they would not have committed you for trial. And I must say that having read all about it, I'm not very surprised. So, I have to ask you very seriously, are they right or are they wrong? Were you one of the men that night? Were you there wearing a stocking mask and wielding a chair leg as a club?'

Bernie Johnson looked furtively about him before replying in a strong cockney accent, 'Oh no, Mr Pearse, I wasn't even there.'

'So, where were you? Have you got a few worthy respectable friends who can give you an alibi?'

'Well... I don' know what you'd call respec'able... There's always Doris Dawkins. Wife of your old client, Dick Dawkins. She's never done time 'erself... only been cautioned for shoplifting... and some time ago that was.'

'Not quite what I had in mind, Bernie. On the good side, they didn't catch you in the act, although there is the absolutely damning verbal admission. But we'll come to that a little bit later on. But apart from that, how could your fingerprints possibly have got onto that chair leg? It has been identified by three witnesses as identical with one of those used in the robbery.'

'Well I *can* help you there, Mr Pearse… as you know, I had just been on an 'oliday to Spain for four weeks, just after the date you gave for this robbery…'

'The prosecution are likely to suggest that you were spending the ill-gotten gains of the contents of the mailbags?'

'Mr Pearse!'

'So, how did your prints get on that chair leg?'

'Well, it was like this… some weeks after they done the bank job. From what I *heard*…'cos as I swear, I wasn't there at all …I was up in Islington having a drink with a mate. Then this bloke, who was a friend of 'is, come over and joined us and we all had a drink to'gever. Well, when it come to near enough closing time this other bloke, 'is name was Albert, said without me asking, as 'ow 'e could give me a lift home in his motor 'cos it 'ad come out he lived round my way. "Yo're on, mate," I said. And he did. Well, what should I see on the back seat of 'is car but this chair leg. So I just picked it up to see what it was. Out of curiosity like. That's what must have done it. It must 'ave been that Albert was one of 'em; that that was the motor that was used and the chair leg I picked up got left be'ind by mistake.'

James Hawkins interjected to ask, 'So, who is your friend Albert… and where can we find him?'

'Not a friend, so much, just a bloke I saw in the pub that night. 'E was a pal of Bill Gurney.'

'And where can we find *him*?'

'Well, you see, I only saw him in the pub that night and I 'aven't seed 'im since.'

'Well then, what about Bill Gurney and where does he live?'

'Well, it's a funny thing but soon after, Bill Gurney come into a lot of money and orf 'e went. To the South of France, for all I know.'

Tam Pearse began to look very serious as he said, 'Unlikelier stories have been accepted by juries I know, but it doesn't sound too promising... so where were you at 3pm on the day in question, 4th March last, since you were not outside Barclays Bank in Camden? Prosecuting counsel is bound to ask.'

'Well, Mr Pearse, that was an awful long time ago... and I couldn't say where I was unless I was sure about it, now could I...? Not to take me oath... and I just can't remember.'

'So what about what you *are said to have said* to the officers in the police car the day they picked you up then...?' He looked down to read from his papers spread out on the desk before him. ' "...I don't mind going down for the motor, but I never rolled the geezer..." Did you say that or didn't you?'

'Well now, Mr Pearse... would I say a thing like that...? I didn't say nothing.' Bernie looked round the room with an injured expression.

The others in the room looked at each other before James Hawkins said with conviction, 'I'm thinking of his record of previous convictions. It's as long as your arm and I do think he must have learned something... would he have said anything like that piece of jargon, which might have been taken straight from the pen of Damon Runyan, or a less good episode of "The Bill"...? No I think not; not in a million years. A confession from Bernie? However strong the evidence, and before seeing any of his lawyers? No way. What do you think Mr Pearse?'

'For the first time since I first opened the brief, I now have my doubts about the result. Because if you never said those words attributed to you, then it must amount to a particularly nasty verbal, and one I should be able to exploit with the jury. It could be a chink in the case for the prosecution, perhaps about the only one. The jury would normally be highly likely to believe the evidence of the two PCs rather than you, but this time they have surely gone just a shade too far. Mr Hawkins, you will do what you can to find anyone who could verify our client's case about the meeting in the pub... Bill Gurney or Albert for instance?'

'Well Mr Pearse, I've had a good try already. I thought that there must be someone who had been in that pub on the night in question, who might remember Bernie. Or who could identify Albert and substantiate Bernie's story, at least a little. I remembered my Gilbert and Sullivan and I was looking for something, anything, which might provide some "merely corroborative detail... to give artistic verisimilitude" to what some might think, was "an otherwise bald and unconvincing narrative". But no such luck.'

The door opened and Challen put his head round it to say urgently:

'I've just heard from the Bailey. The list has really quite collapsed, they've just told me... and Regina versus Bernard Johnson is on in front of the Common Sergeant first thing tomorrow.'

In good time for court next day, Tam Pearse and Patsy Hornby, dressed in wigs and gowns, were sitting on a bench outside Court 2 at the Old Bailey waiting for the case of Regina-versus-Bernard Johnson to be called on for hearing, their briefs in their hands and law books beside them.

Tam Pearse turned to his pretty young pupil to say, 'Not unexpectedly, Mr Hawkins has come up with nothing overnight. A barrister has to accept what his client says is true unless he *knows that it is not. Suspecting his client is lying is not enough.* If it were, why then perhaps my practice would dwindle. But Bernie is the only witness for the defence. It certainly is not a case in which I could afford not to call him to give evidence, thus saving him from all the risks of cross-examination. The prosecution has far too strong a case for any such luxury. Their case will call for an answer and the only person to make that answer must be Bernie himself. And, of course, by me on his behalf, in my speech to the jury...'

'And, of course, as you were saying, there is that one flaw in their case because surely no one is going to believe those stupid words, that admission of guilt he is supposed to have made?'

'Well, it is very little on its own but just possibly, it might be enough... if we play our cards right. We shall have to see how it all goes because it is our duty, if we can, to get an acquittal... and you never know, there may be one or two on the jury with no great love for the police.'

'Well both Mr Hawkins and Bernie himself seem to think that if anyone can do, then it must be you.'

'Very flattering and I can only hope they are right... but you do know who the judge is? It is the Common Sergeant Eustace Beesleigh. I've been before him only once before, when my client went down, when I had thought he stood a reasonable chance of acquittal. Beesleigh has an unfortunate habit of referring to the evidence given by the prosecution with an unctuous respect in his voice saying, without much exaggeration, things like "Well then, members of the jury... you will remember that you have heard the evidence of not one, *but two* police officers, men of some experience in the Force, and one of them a *Sergeant.* You may think that their

70

evidence is *very clear* and that they have *no doubt at all* that it was the defendant that they saw on the night in question. *If you accept their evidence*, and of course (dropping his voice), it is entirely a matter for you, not me, as to whether you do or not, *then* you may think that your task is an *easy one* and that you will have no alternative but *to convict*. But then... sniff... you have the evidence of the defendant himself..." a long pause, and a very pronounced sniff "...that on the night in question he was *far away*, with his friends (sniff), whose names he did not give to the police and neither of whom has been called as a witness in this case... drinking beer in a *Public House*. Well, of course, *if* you believe *that*..." loud sniff "...then, (dropping his voice)... he is entitled to be acquitted." In the case I am talking about, the jury convicted without any hesitation after listening to Eustace... although I felt myself that there must have been at least some element of doubt.'

'So you think that Bernie, who we both think is as guilty as hell, has no chance at all then?'

'Well sometimes, I know, Eustace Beesleigh overdoes it. Juries are not fools. Their members are men and women of the world. Some, who knows, without too much love for Law Courts and police officers. They may see through Eustace's little ways and react against them. They might remember instead all that Eustace will be forced to say, even if somewhat *sotto voce,* about it not being the duty of the defendant to prove that he is innocent, but the duty of the prosecution to prove that he is guilty. And that unless they were satisfied of guilt, they must acquit. Eustace, of course, will be forced to say this, because he knows full well that if he does not and Bernie is duly found guilty, we could go for an appeal to the Court of Appeal. Such an appeal would be sure to succeed since a clear direction from the judge as to the onus of proof lying upon the prosecution, is deemed an essential element in any direction to the jury in any criminal trial. We are living in the days of the court shorthand writer, who records every word said in his notebook.

Patsy thought for a moment before saying, 'The Court of Criminal Appeal would surely be on the watch for any obvious bias on the part of the judge, which might prevent a fair verdict being given?'

'Exactly... but there is no way for the court shorthand writer, to take down a sneer, a sniff or any other inflection of voice. There is not much that can be done by counsel for the appellant by way of mimicry of a senior judge, in the absence of some hard evidence of it. I have heard of a possibility of change in the future. Shorthand writers are highly skilled but expensive to employ. Tape recorders will undoubtedly become the order of the day but no one trusts them yet. They might be quite able to reproduce sneers and other inflections of voice, so that the judges in the Court of Appeal could hear them and draw their own conclusions. It would have to follow very quickly indeed that trial judges would stop doing it, so that much better justice would follow. But they won't come in until after Eustace has retired to write his memoirs. But he might also overdo his digs at Bernie in our case and that could cause a counter-reaction by the jury in our favour.'

'Tam, what do you know about the man who's prosecuting us?'

'Michael Hemmings has been one of the standing counsel here for some years. He has a reputation as a fair man... and, perhaps for that reason, he is a formidable opponent.'

'It was very good of you to get Mr Hawkins to give me a brief as your junior, it is my very first ever,' and Patsy blushed with pleasure as she glanced down at the brief in her hands, her name upon it and bound about with red ribbon.

But then they heard a voice call out from the court behind them:

'Regina versus Bernard Johnson' and they hurried into court and took their places in counsel's row, next to the tall and portentous-looking figure of Michael Hemmings, who sat conferring with his solicitor, who was sitting immediately in front of him in the row reserved for solicitors. They all settled into their seats, opened their papers before them and waited. The Clerk of the Court called for the jury in waiting to come into court to be called individually by name, to take their places in the jury box and then to be sworn to 'well and truly try the several issues joined between Her Majesty the Queen and the prisoner, Bernard Johnson, and true deliverance make according to the evidence'.

The Clerk of the Court rose up and looked carefully round to see that everything was ready; counsel in their places and the prisoner looking as calm and as innocent as it was possible for him to do in the dock, between the two wardens whose duty it was to see that he stayed there, although there was really very little chance that he would try to escape, before reading out the charge on the sheet before him:

'Bernard Johnson, the charge is that on the 4th March last in Camden High Street, at about 12.15 in the afternoon, you with others, not presently before the court, robbed Securicor staff of the sum of £85,000 in security bags they were in the process of delivering to Barclays Bank... how say you? Are you "guilty" or "not guilty" of that charge?'

Now he rose to his feet. Hitching his gown about his lanky figure he began in the time-honoured fashion 'May it please you, M'Lud, in this case I appear to prosecute and the defendant has the advantage of being represented by my learned friend Mr Pearse...' And so the whole prosecution case was detailed. On the 4th March last, at about 12.15 in the afternoon, the usual weekly delivery of funds was being made to the branch of Barclays Bank in Camden High Street, by Securicor staff in one of their employer's vans. After only the second bag had been handed on to waiting bank staff, a black Ford Zodiac, later identified as stolen, came screeching to a halt outside the branch and just behind the stationary Securicor van. 'Three, or some witnesses thought four, men came bursting out of this car,' said Michael Hemmings, '...they were wearing black stocking masks over their faces and so it has not proved possible to identify any one of them by any witness at the scene. They were carrying what appeared to be black truncheons, but these had been later identified as chair legs, of the kind that are screwed into self-assembled, upright chairs. These men, and the prosecution say that Bernie Johnson was one of them, unless, that is, as you may think when you have heard the evidence, he was perhaps the driver. A man who stayed in the car with his head bowed low over the steering wheel while the robbery was actually taking place.'

'The robbers...' continued Michael Hemmings, '...at once attempted to seize the bags carrying the bank's money. There were only two Securicor staff carrying them. One of these was so startled that he allowed the two bags he held to be taken from him. The other managed to hold on. The result was that he received a heavy blow to the head, which so shocked him that he loosened his grip on one bag, but kept hold of the other. Fortunately, the incident left him, although badly shaken, only with some nasty bruising. This was a busy high street, and a busy part of a normal shopping day in Camden. A crowd of shoppers were watching, as you can imagine with dismay and mounting anger. One man had already rushed into a shop and called out "quick 'phone the Police". But on encountering signs of opposition, one of the attackers panicked and started to run. The others saw this and panicked too, carrying away three bags of money. Seeing one of their number run off, the others soon followed, leaving one Securicor man on the ground. The attackers hurled themselves into their car, waiting only feet away with its engine running. The car at once raced off, nearly colliding with passing traffic, just missing an approaching Post Office van and rounded the next corner... to disappear. Three bags of money were stolen which contained, according to the bank's records, no less than £22,600. None of it has ever been recovered.'

'So why does the prosecution say that Bernard Johnson, this defendant, was one of those men? Particularly when you will remember that I have told you that they were wearing stocking masks over their faces?' asked Michael Hemming rhetorically, pausing to look at the jury still listening, Tam noticed uneasily, with rapt attention. He threw out one arm and raised a well-groomed eyebrow in mute enquiry, before answering his own question. 'Because the stolen Ford Zodiac was found abandoned in Whitechapel two days later. Its number D680VCT, had been noted down by three different people at the scene of the crime. Abandoned on the floor of the car, in the back, were three of the black chair legs. You may think that there is little doubt of this,' said Michael Hemmings, 'they have been identified by four of the witnesses I shall call before you, as being in every way identical in appearance to the ones they saw being wielded that day. Although, of course, they cannot be absolutely certain they were the same. But they were found on the floor of the black Ford Zodiac, number D680VCT, and you may think that there is not much doubt about it,' he said fairly. Well, after all, he could afford to be fair, on this point at least. There was no dispute. Tam rose to my feet, anxious to play some part in what was fast becoming a one-horse race.

'M'Lud,' Tam interjected, 'the defendant does not dispute that the chair legs found in the car may well have been used in the robbery that day. He can't say... he wasn't there.'

'Thank you Mr Pearse,' said Eustace, looking all the same far from pleased. Had there been a plea of 'guilty', as he clearly thought there should have been, he'd have been out on the golf course by now, or perhaps at Goodwood, Tam thought. 'I am sure that Mr Hemmings will be relieved to

75

hear that there is one point in the prosecution case, at least, which is not in dispute.'

'And on one of those chair legs, members of the jury,' continued Hemmings... 'were found two fingerprints and one thumb print. They have been identified by officers in the Forensic Department, New Scotland Yard, who I shall call before you, as belonging to the defendant, Bernard Johnson. The chances that they do not are 1.8 million against.' Michael Hemmings paused to give emphasis to his best point, and watched to see what effect it might have. This time, Tam stayed seated. He had no admissions to make. It was not for him to make the prosecution's task any easier. Quite the reverse, and now was not the right time to give any hint of Bernie's, even Tam thought, rather far-fetched explanation about the strange coincidence of his being given a lift in the very same car, so soon after it had been used in the robbery and so soon before the car was found abandoned by the police.

'And that's not all, members of the jury.' Michael Hemmings paused again, standing back, hands on hips, looking at the expectant jury with the faintest of triumphant smiles. 'The police, as you can imagine, kept watch for the defendant but he could not be found in his usual haunts. However, just over four weeks later on 6th April, a police patrol car was travelling towards Hoxton market in Shoreditch. The two officers in the car, both of whom I shall call before you as witnesses in this case, saw the defendant. He was walking along the pavement towards the Town Hall. The driver, PC Gale, stopped the car beside him and his colleague, PC Pryor, shouted out:

'Hey, Bernie, we were looking for you, now we've found you... come over here for a moment, will you...? If you've got a moment to spare that is.'

The defendant... and the officers have no doubt that it was this defendant who now stands before you charged with the robbery in question, at once came across to the car, bent down to the window and said, so that the two officers could clearly hear him, and without any prompting from either of them:

'If it's the blagging in the High Street you're after, I don't mind going down for the motor... but I never rolled the geyser.'

Michael Hemmings translated obligingly for the benefit of the jury.

'If you accept that evidence, members of the jury, you may have no difficulty in accepting also that the defendant, on the 6th April last, was admitting that he had been present at the robbery, accepting that he had been the driver of the stolen car that was used, but denying that he had actually assaulted Mr Higgins, the Securicor employee who suffered the nasty blow to the head, which would be likely to attract a heavier sentence in the event of a conviction in any criminal court.'

Counsel for the prosecution, having dealt with the facts, next dealt with the burden of proof saying, with the manner of a man uninterested in the actual result of the case:

'The prosecution say that there is all the evidence you need to be satisfied of the defendant's guilt, since it matters not if he actually struck Henry Ferguson, the injured man. He is merely charged, as you will remember from having heard the indictment read to you, that he, "On 4th March last, being concerned with men unknown, contrary to the Larceny Act, did rob Barclays Bank of £85,000, the property of the bank". You will take all directions as to the law from the Learned Judge, members of the jury, and not from me. But he is sure to tell you, and the prosecution fully accept, that it is for the prosecution to prove to you that the defendant is guilty and not for him to prove to you that he is not. Further, that if at the end of the trial and having heard all the evidence in the case, you have any doubt in the matter, then Bernard

Johnson, like every other defendant in this country, is entitled to the benefit of that doubt and to be acquitted... but you may feel, at the end of the day, that there is no doubt... and in that event,' Michael Hemmings paused for a moment... 'you will have no option, in accordance with the oaths as jurors that you have taken, but to bring in a verdict of "guilty". I will now call the evidence before you so that you may judge for yourselves.'

Michael Hemmings then called a number of witnesses who had been passers-by outside the Camden Branch of Barclays Bank that day. They described how they had been in Camden High Street at about 12.15 that day and had noticed that a Securicor van was delivering money to the bank. Suddenly a black Ford Zodiac car, registration number D680VCT, had pulled out of a stationary position further down the High Street, and driven up close behind the Securicor van. The driver immediately slumped over the wheel, concealing his face, but one witness said that anyway he had a scarf tied over his mouth so that it was impossible for him to be recognised. Even before the car had quite stopped, other men burst from it. Their faces were hidden by black stocking masks and they were brandishing some kind of black cudgels. One of them seized a money bag from a startled guard almost without resistance. Another of the men tried to pull a money bag from a further guard who hung onto it stoutly. His reward was a blow from the cudgel the attacker held and this caused him to loosen his grasp enough for the attacker to tear the bag away. One witness had immediately rushed into a tobacconist's, the nearest shop, shouting, 'Police... call the police, quick'. Almost as soon as some resistance was shown by Mr Higgins, the men broke off the attack and ran to the waiting car, its doors still open, and this immediately raced off nearly colliding with other traffic. It rounded the corner and was gone. Soon after it had passed the stationary Securicor van, it was effectively out of their sight.

Bank officials were called to prove the counting and dispatch of the money which had been stolen. The two Securicor guards were called and gave their accounts of the robbery. Henry Higgins, the one who had held on to his bags of money and been injured for his trouble, rated a word from the Bench:

'Mr Pearse,' said Eustace, and he hurriedly rose to his feet, '...from your cross-examination of the witnesses called so far, or rather from the lack of it, am I right in assuming that the defence do not contest that there was a robbery at Barclays Bank on 4th March last, more or less as described, whatever is said about your client's involvement in it?'

'That is so, M'Lud, I have asked no questions so far simply because Mr Johnson was not there... so he is in no position to dispute any of the evidence we have heard... *so far.*'

Eustace gave a particularly loud and derisive sniff and turned to the witness:

'Mr Ferguson, I think that everyone in this court, with an interest in upholding justice and the rule of law...' he paused to glance at Bernie sitting impassive in the dock who, he clearly thought, had not... 'will think that you behaved most courageously that day in trying to protect the property of your employers. Please accept our thanks.' There was a general murmur of approval in court.

'Call PC Edward Pryor,' said Michael Hemmings and Tam's interest quickened. Pryor looked a stolid London copper. About middle-aged, he had been around enough to know the ropes well... and all the dodges, Tam thought, as he entered the witness box. Raising the Good Book on high, he intoned as directed by the court usher. 'I swear by Almighty God that the evidence I shall give shall be the truth, the whole truth and nothing but the truth.' Out it all came in a continuous rush. The mark of the professional witness, Tam thought, rather than one who was really believing in what he was saying.

'Are you Edward John Pryor? A constable in the Metropolitan Police?' asked Michael Hemmings with the air of a man who needed reassurance although, if he had read his brief, he must have known it perfectly well.

Pryor agreed that he was.

'On the afternoon of Sunday 6th April, were you on duty with PC Gale in a marked police car in Hoxton market in Shoreditch?'

'Yes, sir.'

'...and did the two of you see anybody you recognised?'

'Yes... Bernie Johnson.' Pryor gestured towards the dock.

'Was he a man known to you before that day?'

'Yes.'

'And did you also know that he was wanted for questioning in relation to the robbery of bank money from Barclays Bank in Camden about a month before?'

'Yes, sir.'

'Did you open the passenger's window while Gale drew up beside him and stopped the car?'

Pryor agreed he had.

'What was said between you...? I think that the Learned Judge will allow you to consult your notebook, if you have it here, and if it contains a contemporary record of the events it describes, made up as soon as possible afterwards.' Hemmings glanced courteously at the judge.

Confirming that he had made up his notebook as soon as possible after the incident, Pryor was given permission and opened the notebook to lay it flat on the ledge of the witness box in front of him.

'I said "Hey Bernie! We were looking for you... now we've found you... come over here will you...?" I didn't need to say anything more because the defendant came over, bent down at my window and said at once...

'"If it's the blagging in the High Street you're after... I don't mind going down for the motor but I never rolled the geezer."' Pryor was still consulting the notebook.

'Then you took him back to the police station and formally charged and cautioned him?' suggested Michael Hemmings.

'Yes, sir, we did.'

'And did he say anything in answer to the charge?'

'No, sir, he said nothing.'

Michael Hemmings gave a satisfied push to his wig, which had slipped a little, pulled his gown about him and sat down. So now it was up to the defence.

Tam Pearse stood up and said nothing while he straightened his wig, tidied his robes and looked at the jury, with a look which seemed to be asking for their confidence, as well as expressing, by means of a raised eyebrow, that there was a good deal more to it all than anyone had heard as yet.

'Did that surprise you, Officer?'

'What, sir?' said Pryor, looking surprised himself.

'Did it surprise you that Mr Johnson said nothing in answer to the charge?'

'No, sir, I can't say it did,' said Pryor still looking puzzled

'It did not surprise you because Mr Johnson is a man of few words, isn't he?' Tam suggested.

'Well, yes, you could say that... as a normal rule,' said the officer, wondering where the trap lay.

'So, you must have been amazed, really amazed, when you stopped him in Hoxton market and, without even having to ask him about it, or mention the incident about which you were making enquiries, he blurts out what the prosecution say is a complete admission to being involved in the Barclays Bank robbery?'

'Well, it does sometimes happen, sir.'

'A guilty conscience, you mean? Or is it,' Tam asked, with all the sarcasm he could manage '...that it just happens that suspects that you are questioning come out with apparently amazing admissions of guilt?'

'Yes, sir, you could say it was a guilty conscience or per'aps he just blurted it out.'

'But not Bernie Johnson, surely?'

'That's what he said,' said the officer stubbornly.

'Every word of it?' Tam Pearse asked, repeating the words with irony and heavy emphasis and reading from the depositions, the written account of the evidence taken down at the earlier hearing of the case in the Magistrates' Court.

'"If it's the blagging in the High Street you're after, I don't mind going down for the motor...?"'

'That's what he said, sir.'

'"...but I never rolled the geezer?"'

'...well I suggest to you, PC Pryor, that when you stopped the defendant, as he agrees you did, he said not a word, just as you agree he said nothing when the charge was

82

read out to him? In fact generally speaking he is a man of very few words.'

PC Pryor did his best to assume an injured air and consulting his notebook said, 'He said just as I said... what I've already given in evidence,' he emphasised.

'You have been consulting your notebook all the time haven't you?' Tam said, '...may I see it?'

With clear reluctance, the officer handed the book down.

'There is no reason why the officer should not consult his notebook and I have given him leave to do so,' pointed out Eustace Beesleigh from his position above the court.

'No, indeed, My Lord, and, with all respect to your Lordship, there is no reason why I should not examine it, and perhaps in due course, with your Lordship's leave, the jury too, might wish to have a look at it.'

'Oh, very well, Mr Pearse, if you really think all this is going to help,' said Eustace looking bored, but Tam had noticed a hint of rising interest in the faces of the jurors sitting opposite to him.

And so the notebook was duly handed down and Tam Pearse had a good look at it. Written neatly and legibly it bore out all that Pryor had said and was dated 6th April, the day of the incident. Tam glanced back in the book and noticed, without much surprise, that the entry before was dated 2nd April and the one after the 5th. Not much for me there, he thought, and handed the notebook back.

'And did you make up that note while the incidents were still fresh in your mind...? In the police station...? But quite independently of anyone else?' he asked politely.

Pryor answered 'yes' without hesitation to each question. Police rules strictly required that, where two or more officers were to give evidence in the same case, then their notebooks should be made up quite independently of any other officer, to obviate any suggestion of collusion between them. And as soon as possible after the event or conversation being recorded. Very sensible it all was, but these strict rules were sometimes honoured more in the breach than in the observance. Police officers lead busy lives, and human frailty applies to them as much as to anyone else.

'What time was it?'

'By the time we'd got back, charged the defendant, listed his possessions, reported to the DI and had a cup of tea, it would be about 6pm, I should think, sir.'

'When did Gale make up his note?'

'Must have been the same time... but in another room.'

'So you did not make up your note in company with PC Gale? Are you quite sure of that...? Take as long as you like to consider before you answer.'

But Pryor answered at once, virtuously and emphatically.

'Quite sure, sir, I was on my own... Gale was in another room. All strictly in accordance with the rules.'

'You see, it is rather strange, because I have a copy of the depositions in this case, setting out what PC Gale said in the Magistrates' Court. The evidence he is also expected to give here, quite soon. It is word-for-word the same as the account you have just given. Not the difference of a single word.'

'We were describing the same event, sir,' Pryor pointed out unctuously.

'Even so... isn't it rather strange that two accounts, that you say were made up quite independently of each other, should turn out to be identical... when you were each writing up your notebooks separately some three hours later?'

PC Pryor now looked a little uncomfortable, but he stuck to his guns. 'It's the truth, sir,' he insisted.

'At that time, did PC Gale have a girlfriend, called Julie Bragg?' Tam asked cautiously. Reg Hawkins, of Messrs Travers-Smith and Dobson, Laburnum Street, Hackney, his instructing solicitors, had been earning his money and making a few enquiries. Easy for him this time because he himself had a girlfriend who worked in the canteen at Shoreditch Police Station

'Yes, he did, sir.'

· 'A bit of a dish was she?'

Eustace leaned forwards at once to protest. 'Really, Mr Pearse...'

Tam Pearse accepted the rebuke and hurriedly substituted '...she was an attractive young woman, was she? and Gale was very keen on her?'

'Yes, I agree with that, but what it's got to do with this case...'

'It has this to do with this case, PC Pryor... Gale was late for his date with Julie that evening wasn't he...? Shoreditch Police Station is in Shepherdess Walk and Julie lived over in the Angel, so Gale wanted to be off? He left it to you to do the necessary that night, didn't he?'

'I don't know what you mean.' said Pryor, looking Tam thought, decidedly apprehensive.

'Then let me be specific,' Tam said, basing himself partly on what Reg Hawkins had told him his girlfriend had told him, perhaps just a little, on hope and speculation.

'What I am suggesting is, that as soon as you got back to the police station, you said to Gale "Right, leave it to me, you hop it" or something like that? ...And he nipped off at once and left it to you to deal with the formalities, including making up your notebook...? What really happened was that several days later, you lent Gale your notebook and he copied it all down...? Word-for-word...? So it is not the independent corroboration of what you have told My Lord and the jury at all, is it?'

'No, no, it wasn't like that...' But Pryor was now looking more than a little bit bothered, a thin film of perspiration had appeared on his forehead. The jury, Tam was pleased to note, seemed to be all attention.

'Mr Pearse,' interjected Eustace Beesleigh, giving Pryor some much needed respite. 'This is not all supposition? You do have specific instructions on which to base this line of cross-examination?'

'Oh Yes! My Lord, I have instructions from my client as to who was present in the police station that night. I also have information, from an independent source, as to certain circumstances at Shoreditch Police Station.' Tam was not going to say more than he had to, and there was no rule of practice or procedure which allowed anybody to look into the brief of counsel for the defence at a criminal trial. The truth will out, they say. Although Tam wasn't at all sure that that would be good for Bernie Johnson, if taken to its logical conclusion. But so far as PC Pryor was concerned, he hoped the old saying might be true. He was not at all displeased with the way things had gone at this stage. Pryor had looked decidedly uneasy and now seemed too obviously relieved as Tam resumed his seat.

'No re-examination, My Lord,' said Michael Hemmings and prepared to call his next witness, PC Gale.

It was now still only 3pm in the afternoon of the first day of the trial, and Tam knew that there would be no chance for PC Pryor to confer with his colleague outside the doors of the court before it was Gale's turn to give evidence. Very well, he looked at him carefully. A lot, perhaps everything would depend on what admissions he could persuade him to make.

PC Gale looked younger and less experienced than his colleague, who Tam judged would have been the leading spirit in any joint enterprise. Did he look just a shade uneasy as he took the oath? Just a little nervous for a man who really was going to tell the truth, the whole truth and nothing but the truth, as he was swearing he would? Well, perhaps, Tam thought hopefully. Gale asked for permission to consult his notebook to remind himself of what had happened. Such was the crowded state of the lists of criminal cases awaiting trial at the Old Bailey in the 1960s that it was now many months since the events of the robbery.

'Certainly you may consult your notebook, if it is a contemporary record,' said Eustace graciously.

And so it all came out. The evidence was, of course, just the same. Word-for-word. Given in a steady voice. Carrying conviction. Until Hemmings sat down and once more it was Tam's turn to cross-examine.

'May I see that notebook?' he asked at once. There was nothing that Gale could do about it but to part with his notebook and hand it down for Tam to examine with anxious attention. There it all was, exactly the same as he had known it would be and dated 6th April 1955, the day of the arrest. And then Tam had the happy thought to turn back to the previous entry...

'You say that you made up your notebook immediately on returning to the police station, not in collaboration with PC Pryor, but in a separate room from him?'

'Yes, sir, I did.'

'And the notebook runs continuously on... you didn't go back and fill in a few pages later on, I suppose... or did you?'

'Oh, no, sir, certainly not!'

Tam handed the notebook back to the court usher to give to the witness.

'Look at your own notebook and find the entry in question, dated 6th April.'

The witness did this and said, 'Yes, sir, I've got it.'

'Now turn to the *previous* page... is that an entry recording your arrest of a man called Jolyon Fothergill, for taking and driving away a motor car, not his property?'

'It is, sir.'

'And that entry, on the *previous* page, is dated too, isn't it?'

'Yes, sir.'

'And what is that date?'

'Well... it's dated 9th April.'

Gale turned a decided shade of pink as he realised what he had just admitted.

'My Lord,' Tam said turning to the judge, 'I ask that this notebook be made an exhibit in the case and that it may now be handed to the jury so that they may see for themselves, and make what they can of a running record where the note of the events relating to this trial are recorded after another event which bears a later date.' Tam could not stop a lurking smile of satisfaction crossing his face. A glance at Michael Hemmings revealed that he was sitting rigidly: his face impassive. Not for him now the slight smirk Tam had noticed once or twice before.

So it was agreed and the Usher passed the notebook to the jury, who passed it among themselves audibly murmuring, one giving a faint snigger, instantly suppressed.

'So how do you explain that, officer?' Tam asked.

'Well I must have got the date wrong... anyone could.'

'Yes, but which date was wrong? The date of your supposed note of the defendant's arrest or the note of your arrest of Jolyon Fothergill? Or are they both equally fictitious?'

There was no reply to this and Tam had not really expected one.

'You didn't get the date wrong at all, did you? The real truth is, that you did not make up your notebook on your return to the police station on 6th April at all, did you? You went out on a date with your girlfriend...? You just borrowed PC Pryor's book some days later and copied down what he'd said, so your evidence is just a repeat of his?'

'No, sir.'

'It is not independent, not your own note at all, is it? Just a copy of what Pryor had written when you both returned to the police station, but you left hurriedly for your date with... was her name not Julie Bragg?'

The witness remained silent, his face no longer pink but looking rather like suet pudding.

'That will be for the jury to say, Mr Pearse,' interjected Eustace Beesleigh, sourly.

'Yes, indeed, My Lord, and I'm sure they will make up their own minds about it,' Tam said with a conspiratorial glance at them.

'As far as the conversation you had with Mr Johnson on the 6th April is concerned, when you stopped him in Hoxton market, the real truth is that he never made any admission at all did he? He never said a word, did he?'

'Oh yes, he did, sir!' Tam hoped that the jury would think that he was looking as shifty and unsure of himself as he did.

'"If it's the blagging in the 'igh Street, you'r after..."' Tam said with heavy emphasis, great sarcasm and his very best attempt at a cockney accent.

89

'He said that…? And "I don't mind going down for the motor… but I never rolled the geyser…" he said that? You'll be telling us next that he afterwards made a handsome contribution to the Police Orphans Charitable Fund.'

'I don't quite follow, Mr Pearse,' interjected Eustace, who, on this point at least, was following the case very well indeed. 'The which fund, did you say?'

'Never mind, My Lord, I'll leave it… I think that the jury has got the point.'

Tam Pearse said this with a courteous bow and resumed his seat, looking round at the dock to see how Bernie was reacting to it all. There he sat with a prison officer at his side, the centre of it all. He was looking quite impassive but had a very faint smile upon his lips. The discomfiture of Pryor and Gale must have been very gratifying for him, Tam thought, not without some satisfaction himself. An apparently hopeless case was certainly going as well as anyone could have hoped at this stage. But he knew that there was still a long way to go. Most cases are at their strongest at the close of one's opponent's case, and before the defence's own witnesses have been exposed to the hostile cross-examination of opposing counsel.

Well, after that, the prosecution formally called evidence of the finding of the Ford Zodiac car RJD 680 in a back street in Hoxton some days later. A witness was called to produce Exhibit 1 in the case. This was a black, ebony-looking chair leg equipped with a screw for attachment to its chair. Three more were produced as Exhibit 2 that had no fingerprints on them, but it was Exhibit 1, which did, and it undoubtedly bore the defendant's fingerprints, the witness said. Then there was the evidence of the fingerprint expert from New Scotland Yard. He had been given the defendant's own fingerprints taken from him for the purpose, he said. This was all admitted by the defence. There was not much point in pointing out that even if the defendant's fingerprints had been taken while he was in custody, specially for the purposes of the case, they had also been on the files of the police for several years past. They had, of course, also set off the search for Bernie which had ended on 6th April in Hoxton market. A defendant's previous convictions and bad character are not admissible in evidence, unless the defence make an attack on the character of some prosecution witness going beyond merely putting the defendant's case to him. Tam Pearse had been very careful to avoid this, having no wish at all that the jury should get to know about the long string of convictions attaching to the name of Bernard Johnson on police records. In courts of law, one played by the rules. Particularly if they happened to be in one's own favour.

The fingerprint expert gave all the usual recital with the jargon of his peculiar expertise. The court heard about the whorls and ridges found on the clear prints on the handle of the chair leg he had been given. He compared them in minute detail with Bernie's own finger and thumbprints, a copy of which he had before him. The chances that the fingerprints on the chair leg had belonged to anyone but Bernie was 1.8 million to one against, he said. Tam sat back and listened to all of this with his eyes half closed and looking as bored as possible. When the witness had finished his evidence in chief, he rose to say:

'No questions, My Lord, there is no dispute that the fingerprints belong to the defendant, and he will give a full explanation of how they got there.'

There was no chance here of submitting that the prosecution had made out no case to be answered. On listening to Michael Hemmings opening speech to the jury, Tam Pearse had thought it sounded all too compelling. He knew at once that he would have to call the defendant himself to give evidence on his own behalf and unfortunately, Michael was no slouch at cross-examination himself.

'Yes, Mr. Pearse?' said the judge politely as Tam rose to his feet.

'My Lord, I shall call the defendant.'

Tam said this with more confidence than he felt and Bernie rose to his feet, and was escorted from the dock to the witness box, to do battle on his own behalf.

Tam took the defendant through his statement with care. He was unable to say preciseiy where he had been, or what he had been doing, on 4th March last. No, he was not in work at the time, but looking for work as a builder's labourer. It was some weeks after this that he had first been asked to say where he had been that day and no, he did not keep a diary. Nor could he remember exactly. It was all so long ago. He might have been visiting some friends in Poplar but he couldn't be sure... and they couldn't remember either... and if he couldn't be sure, he couldn't swear to it now, could he?

'What about Exhibit 1, the chair leg with your fingerprints on it?'

'Well, all I can think of is, I was in this pub in Islington one night about that time, it might have been the 5th or the 6th March, drinking with a friend, when this bloke he knew came over and joined us. Well, we had a few more drinks and this other man, 'is name was Albert, said would I like a lift 'ome 'cos it 'ad come out that we lived fairly close, and 'e'd got a motor round the corner, so 'e'd do me a favour if I liked. So I said, yes I would.'

'Yes, Mr. Johnson, please go on,' Tam said encouragingly.

'Well, I got in the car, then I see these chair legs on the seat beside me. I just picked one up to look at it, to see what it was, really. I thought it might have been some kind of a blackjack, but it was only a chair leg as you can see. So, I put it down again. That must have been it.'

Tam Pearse hurriedly turned to safer ground.

'Do you remember Friday 6th April, the day you were stopped in Hoxton market by those two officers, PCs Pryor and Gale?'

'Yes, I certainly do.'

'Well then, just give My Lord and the jury your own account, in your own words, of what really happened?' Tam asked.

Bar Council rules dictated that no barrister could tell his client what to say, or how to say it. It was for him or her only. Not their lawyers. The only permissible advice was 'tell the truth'. But Tam silently hoped that he would keep it short and not over-elaborate, exposing himself to greater likelihood of being caught out on a trivial detail he need not have mentioned at all.

'Well, it was like this, I was just walking along in the market, minding my own business, when this car drew up alongside and the officer shouted out "over 'ere Bernie". So I went over and leaned down at the window. He said something about a robbery at Barclays Bank in Camden High Street and would I come down to the station and answer a few questions to 'elp them with their enquiries. So I didn't 'ave much option, did I? And I got in the car and when we got to the nick, they took me before the desk sergeant. Then they straight away charged me with being concerned with some other persons unknown, with the robbery of certain moneys from Barclays Bank.'

'You've heard what the officers have both said about a conversation when you leant down beside the police car in Hoxton market, and the admissions you made at that time... what did you really say? Please tell the jury in your own words?'

Bernie did not hesitate. 'I didn't say nothing,' he said emphatically.

93

And he stuck to it. All that Michael Hemmings could do in cross-examination would not shake him. It all sounded believable. On the subject of how his fingerprints got onto Exhibit 1, he was rather less convincing.

'So you were just having a drink with a friend in a public house in Islington one night were you?' asked Hemmings sceptically '...is he here in court?'

'Yes sir, I was, sir, it was The Bull in Duncan Street,' said Bernie with the air of a man who likes to be exact about these things, '... but no sir, Bill Gurney is 'is name but I don't see him here,' and Bernie looked round anxiously as if his friend could still appear.

'The other man, the one you say gave you a lift home, is *he* going to give evidence in this case?'

'No, sir.'

'Well then, what is his name...? And where does he live?'

'You see, that's the trouble, sir, 'e said 'is name was Albert, and that's what Bill Gurney called 'im, but I never knew where 'e lived except 'e said it wasn't far from me.'

'Haven't you thought of asking him to come and help you out in this case?'

'I would if I could, sir', said Ernie piously, '...to 'elp the course of justice, but Mr 'awkins, my solicitor, says 'e can't be found though I know he's tried 'ard enough, and I've 'elped 'im all I can, but that's not much 'cos I don't really know 'im.'

'So, what about the friend you were drinking with in the public house? You must know who he is? Is he going to give evidence to substantiate your story?'

'Oh I know Bill Gurney, sir, but his ship came in, didn't it? He won the big race at Ascot one day, then off he went to the South of France... as soon as he got 'is money and never left no forwarding address neither...'

Well, there it was and Bernie stuck to it throughout a keen cross-examination, saying as little as possible beyond the bare answers to the questions. Perhaps Mr Hawkins, court clerk and outside man to that well known firm of North London solicitors, who were instructing Tam in this case, had done more by way of advice to his client than Bar rules allowed him to do. In any event, the defendant would not be shaken from his story, unlikely as some parts of it sounded to the highly sceptical Michael Hemmings.

Well then, the evidence was over, since Tam had no other witness to call. Michael addressed the jury laying stress on the defendant's clear connection with the crime by virtue of the fingerprints on the chair legs which had been used, and his confession to having been at least involved in some way, made to the two police officers in Hoxton market. It was Tam Pearse's right for the defence to address the jury last, before the judge's summing up to them.

'Members of the jury,' he said, hitching his robe about him and fixing his eyes upon a juror in the front row who, he thought, seemed to have been following the case with close attention. He had actually sniggered when Tam had facetiously asked PC Gale if he was suggesting that Bernie had offered to make a contribution to the Police Orphans Charitable Fund. 'In this case, as in every other in this country, it is for the prosecution to prove the guilt of the defendant and not for him to prove his innocence... this means that you must believe that the case for the prosecution is the truth. Not only part of it is the truth, but all of it. If you have *any* real doubts about *any* really important point, then the defendant is undoubtedly entitled to the benefit of your doubts and you *must* acquit him. Think hard and think particularly of the evidence of the two police officers upon which this prosecution is founded...'

'...do you really believe that this defendant... look at him.' Tam pointed to Bernie, sitting immobile and mute in the dock. '...*can you* really believe that he actually said, "If it's the blagging in the High Street you are after... I don't mind going down for the motor... but I never rolled the geezer"?' The note of incredulity in his voice was striking some high and strident decibels, but some members of the jury were looking very thoughtful indeed. '...because that is the very foundation of the case for the prosecution, isn't it? If you cannot believe that, then you can't believe any of it, can you? Think of those words when you retire to consider your verdict. Savour them. But did this defendant really say them? Or anything like them? Most importantly, if you disbelieve the prosecution on this, then you can't just pick and choose some of it to believe, some of it to be outrageous lies; you must remember your oaths as jurymen and women, to try the case according to the evidence. You must acquit.' Tam sat down reasonably happy with the way things had gone and waited to hear what Eustace would say.

Well, he said it all. Of course, it was on the face of it, a very strong case for a verdict of 'guilty'. There was not only the evidence of the fingerprints on the chair leg but also the clear admission of the defendant's involvement *if* that verbal was believed to be true. Eustace himself clearly had no doubts about it at all. 'You have heard the evidence of those two police officers, members of the jury,' he said, the clarity and earnestness of his tone a clear reminder that the evidence of the police was, in his view, in a special category of value. '...then, of course, you have heard the defendant himself give evidence...' The sniff was pronounced. 'He denies it all.' He did not quite say 'well he would, wouldn't he?' But did he have to? '....the defendant says that he was elsewhere that afternoon,' sniff, '...but he can't remember quite where. He has explained how, he *says*, his fingerprints came to be found on Exhibit 1 in this case, the chair leg in question...' double sniff, '...but the men who *he says,* could substantiate his

96

story, *can't be found*. We have not heard or seen them, when they might have been here to help their friend.'

And so it went on. Until he got to his direction on the onus of proof in criminal cases.

'...remember, members of the jury, that in this, as in all criminal cases, it is for the prosecution to prove to your satisfaction that the defendant is guilty and not for him to prove that he is innocent. If you have any *real* doubt about his guilt, then you must return a verdict of "not guilty".'

This was all very fair. But it had to be because it was all being taken down verbatim by the court shorthand writer. The fact that this part of the summing up had been in a lower voice than the rest would not appear on the transcript of the shorthand note. Nor would the sniffs and grimaces of distaste that had accompanied the summing up whenever he was referring to the case for the defence. But had he gone too far? Tam wondered as Eustace finished with a final admonishment that the jury must all be agreed upon a verdict, if they were to return one at all.

And so the jury retired to the jury room, but before going one of them got hesitantly to his feet and said:

'My Lord, may we take the police officer's notebook with us to look at it?'

'Oh, very well,' said Eustace, looking none too pleased.

In the coffee room a few minutes later, Tam Pearse went up to the tall figure of Michael Hemmings.

'Well, that's one you should win, I should think?' Tam said as Hemmings sipped at a cappuccino.

'I'm not so sure,' he replied. 'Eustace piled it on a bit strong, I thought, after I had been all sweet and reasonable, and moderate beyond belief.'

97

'Strange you should say that,' Tam replied. 'I too have just a glimmering of hope.'

After barely half an hour, both counsel were called back to court on hearing that the jury had agreed upon a verdict. Half an hour is too short a time, Tam thought. It usually meant a verdict of 'guilty', since if there were any doubt, it was usually the subject of much argument among the jury and consequent delay. As against this, he noticed with rising hope, the members of the jury were turning to look at Bernie Johnson as they returned to their seats in the jury box. This is a well-recognised sign that they are going to acquit, otherwise they would be likely to avoid his eyes. But, of course, there are exceptions to every rule, Tam thought.

'Members of the jury,' said the Clerk of the Court rising to his feet importantly. 'Have you appointed one of your number to be your foreman, as My Lord directed you?'

The man who had asked to have the notebook rose to his feet and admitted it was he.

'Are you agreed upon your verdict?' asked the clerk.

'My Lord, we are.'

'And do you find the defendant "guilty" or "not guilty" as charged in the Indictment?'

'My Lord, we find him "not guilty".'

'And is that the verdict of you all?' persisted the clerk.

'It is.'

There was no cheer from any friends of Bernie Johnson in the public gallery. Did he really have any friends, Tam wondered. Only Pryor, of the two police officers, was still in court, and he avoided Tam Pearse's eye as he glanced in his direction. Tam's application for Bernie's release inevitably succeeded. A few minutes later, he was having a final word with him outside the court as the members of the jury hurriedly made off, their duty done for that day, at least.

'Well that was a turn up for the book, Mr Pearse,' said Bernie. 'Thank you very much indeed.'

'Fiat justitia et ruant coelum... let justice be done though the heavens fall,' Tam said sententiously translating, since he thought that Bernie might be a bit rusty on his Latin.

A wintry smile twisted the mean lips just for a moment before he replied:

'Well, you could say that, Mr Pearse... on the other 'and... you could say... well, some you win... and some you lose... you could say that, now couldn't you?'

And with Mr Hawkins in close attendance, he hurried off in the direction of El Vino's, that well-known watering hole in nearby Fleet Street, for the lawyer and his client wishing to celebrate or to drown their sorrows.

Demonstrably True

'Consider what you think justice requires, and decide accordingly. But never give your reasons; for your judgement will probably be right, but your reasons will certainly be wrong.'

This was the advice given by Lord Mansfield, Lord Chief Justice to the judges of the Queen's Bench Division, and Tam Pearse was reminded of it when, after several years at the Bar he became a Recorder of the Crown Court, which was an office peculiar to this country, when a barrister becomes a part-time judge but may continue to practise as a barrister, when not actually sitting as a Recorder. So it could be said he has the best of both worlds, because when sitting as a Recorder, he is accorded all the deference that his colleagues and everyone else accords to the judges. And when not sitting, why then, he just gets on with the job he has come to love, of representing all the world of litigants, be they criminals trying to avoid yet another conviction on their already murky criminal record, or bankers chasing a City magnate who is also one of their defaulting customers. But the time in question was some years before this, at a time when Tam's practice was beginning to burgeon from the early days when the best he got was a dock brief and a small fee. It was on a sunny June day when Challen, his senior clerk, came into his room in chambers at 6, Damson Court, The Temple, where he was busy doing his paperwork. That is to say, learning all about the facts of a case he was about to undertake in court, or to give advice on those facts which might avoid the need to go into court at all.

'Your case of Murphy Brothers versus Kingston Construction Limited is warned for hearing for Monday before the Official Referee, as you know, and it should in fact be heard on that day... Mr Pullen of Terrence O'Connor and Co, has asked for a final conference and I've got them all coming to see you this afternoon at 4 o'clock.' Challen managed to look even more like some unctuous cleric or suave butler than usual, as he said this. Tam knew already that he was pleased that he had managed to persuade Patrick O'Connor, his instructing solicitors in the case, to come to his chambers rather than certain others in King's Bench Walk. 'Harry Wolf's name is on the pleadings. He signed the defence... do you happen to know if he is going to do it himself?'

Harry Wolf was a very busy 'junior' at the time. In other words he had not yet 'taken silk' and become a QC. In fact, legal etiquette did not allow him to, since, at the time, he was 'Treasury Devil' for civil work. This meant that he had an official position in government legal circles, while still carrying on his own practice at the Bar. If he needed a 'Leader', it would likely be the attorney or the solicitor-general, since the case would inevitably be concerned with government business. Not only had he received this official accolade as a sign of high approval, but Harry also had a well-earned reputation for being good at his job, including his work in compensation cases such as this, when he would usually find himself briefed for the employer.

'John Dawson, his clerk, says he's available and wants to do it... John seems to think he might be on a winner... even had the nerve to ask if we wanted to settle... But I soon put him right on that, sir,' and Challen hurried out. Lunchtime called him, Tam thought.

101

The case concerned was a 'building claim'. These were cases usually involving the building trade and often dealing with long and tedious matters of detail, on the quality or the cost of a construction of a substantial building, or technical detail about some electrical or engineering matter. They were assigned to a special judge, an 'Official Referee'. Seated in a corridor far above the main hall of the Royal Courts of Justice, these hard-working judges were experts at their trade. They sometimes became a little involved in the case before them, making use of their own knowledge obtained from hearing many similar cases. But there were, of course, expert witnesses available. Not many prudent parties to such a case, nor their solicitors, would go into battle in a contested matter without an experienced expert, skilled in the particular area involved, whatever it might be. But in Murphy Brothers versus Kingston construction, Tam did not have the benefit of any such luxury as an expert witness.

The claim concerned the plastering of a considerable housing estate on the Kingston side of Richmond Park. Tam's professional clients, Terrence O'Connor were, as their name surely implied, concerned very much with the Irish, expatriate community in London. And very often with workers in the construction industry who had fallen off buildings or otherwise injured themselves. Not, of course, because of their own carelessness, but because of some breach of the building regulations, which strictly regulated building work, and the safeguards which had to be taken by the contractors. A breach of these on the part of the employees would almost inevitably be alleged by the client, well advised by Terrence O'Connor, to have caused the accident in question, founding the claim for compensation for personal injury. The legendary Terrence O'Connor himself came from Ireland. All his partners and most of his staff had originated there. Almost every client they produced for Tam seemed to have come from Ireland too. Like calls to like, and Irishmen in London seemed to be naturally drawn to their compatriots when they were in trouble; besides which

O'Connor's had an excellent reputation for success in claims for compensation for personal injuries incurred at work. It had always been a wonder to Tam, not being Irish himself, that they ever came to him. But they did, and had done so with satisfying frequency ever since he had had a few successes for them in the courts. Not least, the one in which he had obtained planning permission for the use of a sports ground at Sunbury for the London Irish Rugby Football Club. Then, his reputation began to run very high with Terrence O'Connor.

The claim Tam was about to discuss with his clients, concerned payment for the work they had done in plastering the 96 houses on a new estate being erected by Kingston Construction on land close to Richmond Park, on the Kingston side of it, the Rockingham Estate. Although there had been a few payments on account, the bulk of their final bill of several thousand pounds remained unpaid. Not because Kingston Construction could not pay, but because they would not. Soon after the work had been completed, some cracks had begun to appear in the façades of some of the houses which had been constructed. Consternation spread, as did the appearance of more and more cracks in more and more houses. If the work done by Murphy Brothers was so clearly defective, Kingston Construction were certainly not going to pay them the rest of their account. But Tam's clients did not agree. The plasterwork they had done had been to their usual high standard. If cracks had appeared, it was no fault of theirs, they said. The simple claim for money owed under the contract was met with a denial that any money was owed, since the standard of the work done was so poor, and a counter-claim for a vast sum was made for loss of profit on the sale of the completed houses. Some of these had already been sold and not all had shown the dreaded cracks. But, inevitably, the word had got about and nearly half of them remained unsold because of it. Not only were Murphy Brothers left with a large, unpaid bill, which they couldn't afford, but with a very large claim being made against them.

'It's more money than we can possibly afford and if this case goes down, we shall go bust,' said Mr Bryan Murphy, as he sat with his brother, Patrick, on the other side of Tam's desk that afternoon.

'Have you read the report of Mr Armstrong, the defendant's expert witness?' Tam asked.

'We certainly have and it's a lot of bunk, for all of his FRICS and his Bachelor of Arts degree. He can't know anything at all about plastering.'

'Well he does seem to be very well qualified... on paper, at least', Tam pointed out. 'As you know, his report says that the cause of all the trouble was that you were using too strong a mix for your plaster.'

'It was 6:1 sand and cement, the same as we always use for fascia work,' replied Patrick Murphy, with the look of the craftsman explaining his mysteries to a novice.

'And you are quite sure that you don't want to call in an expert witness yourselves to confirm all of that?' Tam asked 'It's a bit late in the day... but even so, I'm sure that we could find someone. Perhaps someone else in the trade that you are on good terms with?'

'Now, Mr Pearse, to be sure, expert witnesses cost money and that's in short supply with us right now. And all because of this case. But anyway, we are our own experts... We've both been in the trade for more than thirty years, man and boy... we used the right mix for the job. If it turned out badly then it couldn't be down to us. And Mr Jeavons, the Kingston Foreman and Clerk of the Works, was there the whole time and could see just what we were doing.'

'But being independent sub-contractors and experts in your own right, as you say, the Kingston foreman might probably have felt that he would leave it to you to get on with the job in your own way?'

104

'Well, that's true, to be sure, he was a sensible man and he would have been in the right of it... but we'll still just give our own evidence and the trut' will be sure to come out.'

Patrick nodded in agreement. They clearly had a lot of faith in British justice and Tam only hoped it was not going to be misplaced. He would have been a good deal happier himself, in a case involving an expertise that he did not possess himself, to be able to rely on an expert. Someone with experience and qualifications to rival those of the defendant's expert. Someone for Tam to lean on a bit as he suspected that Harry Wolf would lean on Mr Theodore Armstrong, FRICS, BA.

Monday morning found Tam bustling over to the High Court from chambers, Edward, the junior clerk, was in attendance to carry his few books and his blue bag, the traditional receptacle for the barrister's gown and his wig box.

'Morning, Mr Pearse,' said Tom, the robing room attendant. 'It's big stuff today I hear, Mr Wolf on the other side is it?'

'The bigger they are the harder they fall, Tom,' Tam said, with more apparent courage than personal conviction, as he slipped into the robe that was obligingly held out for him.

'Did I tell you the story of the Scottish duchess taking on some new gamekeepers?' asked Tom. He and his colleague, Charles, were the biggest raconteurs in legal circles. Their forceful, cockney characters, helpful ways and ready wit had endeared them to generations of barristers, and earned them both MBE.s from the grateful Lord Hailsham when he became Lord Chancellor.

On receiving Tam's polite denial, he continued.

'Well the duchess was interviewing two men for the job of gamekeepers. After some preliminary discussion as to what they would be required to do on the vast Highland estate, they were rather surprised to hear her say "now lift your trouser legs and let me see your calves", but they did as she asked with a self-conscious air. "Excellent", said the duchess, "His Grace likes the outdoor men to take a turn as extra footmen if there is a large dinner. It means wearing stockings and knickerbocker trousers so the shape of your calves has to be acceptable, but yours look very good. Now just show me your particulars…"

'A few minutes later the two men were walking disconsolately down the driveway; one of them turned to the other and said, "You know we'd have got that job… if you hadn't been so bloody ignorant".'

Tom laughed immoderately at his own joke and Tam gave an appreciative titter before turning to adjust the bands under his winged collar in the mirror, and putting on his wig. Tom held out the gown for him to shrug on to his shoulders and he was ready. Out through the corner of the robing room, to the stairs leading to the lift and so to the Official Referees' courts high above the Central Hall of the Royal Courts of Justice, and in particular to Court 51, which had been assigned for the trial of Murphy Brothers vs Kingston Construction Ltd.

Here Tam saw Mr Pullen of Patrick O'Connor's with the Murphy Brothers, his clients, and Fergus O'Reilly, the Murphy foreman. This was the moment when settlement of the case might occur. For reasons never fully understood by a sceptical public, a large number of cases settle at the doors of the court just before the case is due to start. Settlement means a formal agreement by the parties to the dispute to end it on agreed terms. Each side must give way a bit and accept rather less, or give rather more, than he had really hoped for, in order for this to be a practicable proposition. But in exchange for this disappointment, each knows that if he is not going to win outright, he will at least not lose everything with the expensive certainty of being ordered to pay the other side's costs as well; such disaster occurring, perhaps, because of some unfortunate lapse by a key witness. Or perhaps because of some personal quirk of the judge trying the case unknown to anybody.

There are good reasons why settlement so often takes place so late, after a hurried discussion, while everybody is waiting for 10.30am and the judge to arrive to make a start, and, for other reasons, probably not so justifiable, but no less compelling. The first good reason is that it is only when everybody is standing outside that both counsel can be really sure which judge is actually going to try the case. For some judges are well known as 'plaintiffs' judges', as opposed to many others equally well known as 'defendants' judges'. It is an unfortunate fact of life that some judges are predisposed to one side or the other, perhaps because they mostly appear for plaintiffs or for defendants when they had been at the Bar themselves. Perhaps because some relation had either been a distinguished building contractor or, on the other hand, had had a nasty experience at the hands of one... who knows? But it is so.

But whether a plaintiffs' judge or a defendants' judge, all are equally pleased if the long and possibly tedious case listed for them to try settles at the last minute. It may mean that another case is hurriedly transferred to their court; but if none is available... then it could mean going home early, or a day at the races, or Wimbledon for the tennis. The less meritorious reasons for late settlements were mostly down to human frailty. Only the urgency of an imminent hearing will shock some dilatory solicitors' clerks into going through all the papers so that their principals, and counsel in the case, can get down to a thorough consideration of it, and the necessary assessment as to what the chances of success and failure really are. Who knows? Perhaps sometimes counsel is at fault, and it was only last night that he had really read his brief with all the essential facts of the case at last assembled for him, for the first time.

But in this case there seemed to be no possibility of any compromise. The Murphy Brothers were not prepared to take a penny less than the sum they had estimated for the work, the amount of the account they had rendered. They needed the money. And, as they told Tam, they had already cut their charges to the minimum to get the job in the first place, much as they now wished it had gone to a rival. On the other hand the defendants had suffered a considerable financial blow because of the unsold houses. In addition, they faced possible legal action from buyers who now had cracked façades to their homes and, of course, the defendants had also suffered a humiliating loss of their good reputation. They were in no mood to pay and admit defeat at this late stage.

A hurried word with Harry Wolf confirmed that his clients had no offer to make. They wanted to succeed on their own counter-claim. This asked for damages for breach of contract, in that the plasterwork in question had been so badly done that it would all have to be re-done. There was also enormous consequential loss in the way of loss of profit on the sale of the houses on the Rockingham Estate, as well as an indemnity in respect of existing, as well as future, claims upon Kingston made by purchasers of the houses. And so everyone made their way into Court 51 and took their seats.

'Court rise,' intoned the usher and everyone dutifully rose to their feet to greet the entrance of His Honour Elfyn David, Official Referee, and a good judge too, in the esteem of the practitioners who appeared in his court, since he was a master of the intricacies of the complicated cases which came before him, and had great patience with both the counsel and the witnesses appearing before him.

'Yes, Mr Pearse?' he asked and Tam rose to his feet to make his opening address.

'The facts of this case concern a large housing development close to the Kingston side of Richmond Park in Surrey,' Tam explained. 'The plaintiffs are plastering sub-contractors and the defendants are the main contractors. The development was to build 96 houses of various descriptions, but three main types. There was a degree of difference between the three types, but all of them involved the construction of a white plaster façade over the front of each building. The work progressed over many months but was nearing completion by the summer months of last year. It was being conducted under the overall supervision of Mr Jeavons, the defendant's Clerk of Works and, so far as the plastering was concerned, the supervision of Mr Fergus O'Reilly, the plaintiff's foreman, and the Murphy brothers themselves who are not above helping out in the work if things get a bit slack in the office. I shall be calling all of them as witnesses for the plaintiffs.

'The plastering work caused no problems for my clients and the work continued as each house was finished over the months. Part-payments were made by the defendants from time to time, · but the sum claimed by the plaintiffs, £1,265,950 together with interest at the statutory rate, remains unpaid. The work on the 96 houses in the estate was all completed, so far as the plastering was concerned at least, by May last year but the final account has remained unpaid ever since. Your Lordship will have read the pleadings and will see that the excuse raised by the defendants for non-payment, and the foundation of their considerable counter-claim, is their assertion that certain cracks, which have appeared in the fascias of some 39 of the houses, were caused by the use of plaster by the plaintiffs of too strong a mix.'

'Yes,' Mr Pearse, I have read the papers in the case, of course, and I was struck by the report of Mr Theodore Armstrong, who has given evidence in this court several times before,' Tam looked round and saw Armstrong sitting beside the defendants' solicitors in the row immediately behind Harry Wolf, a virtuous and self-satisfied smile was flickering across his face. 'Oh, dear!' Tam thought. 'It looks as if they know each other well.'

'But I haven't come across any report from an expert witness on behalf of the plaintiffs?'

The learned judge was clearly a bit put out about this. It was often possible for a judge to suggest that the two experts should go outside the court and discuss their differing reports to see if they might reach agreement on at least some of the points at issue between them. This itself quite often resulted in complete agreement and the end of the case, with no need, as Tam cynically thought, for the judge to listen to all the tedious evidence, noting it all down for the detailed judgement that would be required from him, and with no possibility that his decision might be annoyingly overturned later by the Court of Appeal.

Tam explained that he was not going to rely upon any expert witness; the plaintiffs were their own experts in view of their long experience in the building trade, and their own great experience as expert plastering sub-contractors, well known to the defendants, and the reason no doubt that they had been taken on to do the job in the first place. But he could see that this was not going down too well with Elfyn David. He might profess to be an expert himself on almost every aspect of all the different cases that came before him. He might differ from the professional experts from time to time, but he was used to there being an expert on each side and seemed a little put out.

'Oh, very well, Mr Pearse,' he said. 'You know how to conduct your own case best, of course.' But Tam was not even too sure of that himself since he, too, would have liked to have had the comfort of being able to rely upon a suave, experienced, well-qualified expert like the smug Mr. Theodore Armstrong. Firmly suppressing any doubts he had himself, however, he started to call his witnesses with, he hoped, an air of confidence.

It all seemed very simple. Bryan Murphy gave evidence, and an impressive witness he seemed. He boasted of no qualifications, of course, save for long experience. He had after all, been doing the job for over thirty years, as his father had before him. He had no doubt about the correct mix of sand/cement for fascia work. The mix used was 6:1. It was what they always used. It was the right mix.

'But a mix of 7:1 should have been used according to the evidence that the defendants are likely to give?' Tam suggested.

'Well, Mr Pearse, the truth of the matter is...' emotion was bringing out a broader inflexion to his already pronounced Irish accent.

'7:1 is far too weak. We would never use it at all. Not for a job like this one. T'wouldn't be right.'

Patrick Murphy gave evidence to the same effect, and so did Fergus O'Reilly. Harry Wolf cross-examined them all putting to them that a mix of 6:1 was far too strong and allowed no room for any give in the plaster at all. Of course he made great play with the clear and categorical wording of the report of Mr Theodore Armstrong; his long experience and his undoubtedly impressive qualifications; his clear statement that a mix of 6:1 was much too strong for fascia work. That to use such a mix was asking for trouble. Trouble of exactly the description that had in fact occurred in this case... that it might cause the fascia to exhibit cracks. And all of this within a short space of time as had happened, and was happening, to the houses on the Rockingham Estate on Kingston Hill. In fact, it was the cause of all the trouble, when everyone would surely agree that 7:1 should be the answer, suggested Harry Wolf to each witness in turn, reading again and again from the impeccably printed lines of his expert's report.

'But how much plaster work has he actually ever done himself?' whispered Bryan Murphy in my ear from his seat just behind me 'has he ever even mixed up some plaster of 7:1... or 6:1, for that matter or anything at all? And *give* in the plaster?' Bryan was scandalised. 'Plaster isn't supposed to *give*. There shouldn't be any movement for it to give to.' Tam had to admit to himself that it didn't seem likely that Mr Armstrong had ever plastered as much as a single brick; well, not for himself.

Only once did Fergus O'Reilly allow his guard to drop a fraction. After all, it wasn't his money that was at stake. He was a man giving his evidence on oath, anxious to be exact in every detail. He admitted that he had heard of such a mix being used, but he had not used it himself. Murphy Brothers never did. 'Might it have been better if they had used it?' He couldn't really say. Perhaps it might have been. He couldn't really be sure. 'And if a mix of 7:1 had been used...? Might it not have been that no cracks would have appeared at all, and that all would have been as well as the marriage bell?' asked Harry, uncharacteristically allowing an allegorical phrase to intrude in his cross-examination. Fergus O'Reilly admitted hesitantly that he could not swear, not on his oath, that it could not have been. Tam's heart sank; things were not looking too rosy already, and the court had yet to hear the evidence of the defendants.

Harry Wolf opened his case upon the lines that by this time were very clear. He started to call his witnesses. It was just before the lunch break on the third day of the case that he called Theodore Armstrong, who was duly sworn and presented his much quoted report to the court with a flourish.

'Well, I think that will be a convenient moment for us to rise for the luncheon break... before you start your cross-examination, Mr Pearse? Then you can consider the matter again with your clients over lunch,' he said kindly. But Tam was left with the nasty feeling that he had already reached a view of the matter, even if only provisional... why else had he suggested that he might consider the matter again?

Bryan Murphy was no fool, as Tam had been trying to suggest to the judge throughout the hearing of the case. He came over to him as soon everyone had left the court.

'It don't look too good, Mr. Pearse?' he asked anxiously. 'He seems to be very keen on this expert's report that we don't have?'

'Well I did suggest we should get one, if you remember,' Tam reminded him, 'but if it was not the strength of the plaster mix which caused these cracks, then what was it?'

Strangely enough no one had ever asked this question before and it certainly did not seem to have occurred to the Murphys' to think of it themselves. But we had been hearing all morning from the defendants' witnesses about the awful cracks which had already appeared on the fronts of 39 of the houses. One of the new owners had appeared for the defendants to describe them in gory detail. One had come out above his new kitchen sink, all stainless steel and shining. It was big enough for his wife to stick into it the milkman's bill to remind her to pay it.

'Well, sir, there is only one thing that could have done it... and it's nothing to do with us either,' he added hurriedly. The modern frenzy with compensation neurosis was only just starting at the time, but Bryan Murphy might have been able to foresee a doubtful future for his firm if this claim were to succeed. Word would get about in the trade, that was for sure. He continued, 'It could only be the foundations. I've seen it only once before in all these years and that was long ago. But if they didn't dig the foundations deep enough... or if the ground itself was bad, say a tip had been filled over like... why, that would do it.'

'But how could you possibly tell about that? You'd have to take the houses down... and we couldn't possibly... not in the middle of the trial.'

113

'Well, it would be a lot easier than that, Mr. Pearse, you would only need to take off some pieces of the façades and then, if that was the cause of it all, to be sure, you'd be bound to find that there were cracks in the brickwork underneath.'

He went off in search of a hurried sandwich towards the bar, which was already doing brisk business in the crypt of the Law Courts. After all, he had given his own evidence already and he needed to limber up... to finding consolation or, just possibly, to starting an amazing celebration of success just when all seemed lost? Tam wondered as he considered what he had just said and how best to play his best, it seemed his only, possible trick. But he thought he needed to talk to Bryan again before he started to cross-examine Theodore Armstrong. He needed to be sure before taking such a very big gamble which could misfire disastrously. He reminded himself that it has been said by some great barrister of the past that 'compared with litigation, roulette is a game of skill'. After lunch, as 2 o'clock and the recommencement of the court's business fast approached, Tam Pearse waited anxiously for Bryan Murphy outside Court 51. He was late but, at last, he came looking, Tam thought, as if he might indeed have been enjoying the hospitality of Mr Pullen of Terrence O'Connor's, and his many buddies at the crypt bar.

'Tell me Mr Murphy,' Tam said, 'it's very important... If I could persuade them to take some samples of plaster off one of the affected houses... you say that, if the cause of the trouble was the foundations... you would be bound to see cracks in the underlying brickwork?' Tam needed to be absolutely sure that he had got it right.

'Sure and so you would,' he confirmed.

'Well, things don't look too good at the moment, as you said before lunch, but if I could somehow persuade them to do that, and it proved that the brickwork was sound, it might rebound upon you... because they would know then that there wasn't anything else left for it but bad plastering. We might be sunk properly.'

'Well, there is nothing wrong with our plastering... that's a 'ting that I'm as sure of as I'm sure that I'm standing here... So you go ahead, Mr Pearse. Get them to take it off, if you can... but I don't know how you are going to do it.'

Well Tam was not at all sure either, but he thought he would have a try with the very self-assured Mr Armstrong, who was just about to re-enter the witness box to resume his evidence.

'Now, Mr Armstrong,' Tam began, 'we've all read your report and noted your qualifications which *look* impressive, and your considerable experience... as an expert witness, giving evidence in courts of law, like this one... but when did you yourself last do any actual plastering on a building site like this one?'

It was taking a risk, of course, but Tam thought not much of one, as Theodore Armstrong admitted that he never had.

'So, everything that you have been saying about the correct mix for plaster on fascias is based upon the theory but not the *practice* of the art?'

As he admitted that that was so, Elfyn David interjected, unhelpfully Tam thought:

'Well, of course, you could say that of most expert witnesses, Mr Pearse.'

'Indeed you could, M'Lud... even of experts as well qualified as Mr Armstrong, whose evidence, your Lordship will remember, is in direct contrast to that of the men with practical experience that your Lordship has heard giving evidence for the plaintiffs.'

'Well now, Mr Armstrong,' Tam said turning back to the witness. 'Are you really certain of the evidence you have given... that the cause of the trouble was too strong a mix of the plaster? Is there no other cause that you can think of, for the appearance of the cracks we have heard about, and seen in the photographs that have been produced?'

Armstrong looked puzzled. 'None that I can think of,' he said at last.

'Well, what about the possibility that the foundations of these buildings had been so badly constructed, that there was subsidence? Perhaps because there had been insufficient investigation about the site itself... There could, perhaps, have even been some land in-filling in the past?'

'Well, of course... that might have caused a problem,' he admitted hesitantly, '...that is, if there was actual subsidence.'

'Are you calling evidence to support this suggestion, Mr Pearse?' interjected Elfyn David, looking interested.

'If your Lordship would kindly bear with me for a few moments more,' Tam temporised.

'Mr Armstrong, if the problems have all been caused by faulty foundations, then am I right in thinking... that the cracks showing in the photographs Exhibits D1 to D14... would be mirrored by similar cracks in the brickwork on the front of the buildings that they were covering?'

'Yes, that would certainly be the case,' he admitted.

'You have no doubt about that at all?'

'No, sir, no doubt about it at all... if the cause of the problem was the faulty foundations, then that would show in cracks in the underlying brickwork.'

'And it would be an easy matter to take off some small sections of some of the fascias, so that we could all go down to Kingston and see for ourselves?'

'Yes, it would.'

'Then would it not be a question for His Lordship, as to whether to accept the evidence of yourself and the other witnesses for the defendants on the one hand, or the evidence of the plaintiffs on the other? It wouldn't be a question of theory at all would it... but a question of fact that we could all see for ourselves?'

He now looked more hesitant, but agreed that that would be one way of testing the matter, without doubt.

'...and the only way of being really sure?'

Tam persisted and reluctantly the witness agreed, adding, 'But I have no doubt that the mix of the plaster was too strong.'

'I know that is what you think... the whole of the defendants' case is based upon it... but it would not take as long as an hour or so, for a few men to go along and hack off some specimens of plaster, where there were cracks showing, and find out for sure what was underneath. It could be done this evening, under the supervision of representatives of both the parties, and the Clerk of the Court, too, if his Lordship wanted that?'

He had to agree that that was so, but added...

'Of course, it is not for me to say... they are not my houses you are talking about...'

'But for your part, Mr. Armstrong, would you he happy for that to happen... right now?'

'Yes... I'd be quite happy,' he said after only a moment's hesitation. Well, he could hardly say anything else, Tam thought happily and turned to the judge.

'My Lord... I wonder whether the defendants would agree to this course...? After all, the proof of the pudding?'

Tam Pearse sat down and looked at Harry Wolf with as much significance as he could. He was sitting impassively with his arms folded in counsel's row beside him, watching proceedings closely. Now he turned to take some hurried instructions from his clients. No doubt they were all in a considerable dilemma, Tam thought. If his suggestion were to be refused at this stage, it would seem that the defendants were rejecting what had been admitted to be a clear way of finding out the real truth; that they had no faith in their own case or their own expert.

'Well, of course, My Lord, my clients are only anxious to be as helpful as possible...'

'Very well, Mr Wolf.'

Elfyn David glanced at the clock, which showed only 2.35pm, so with a bit of luck he might be home in time to watch the racing at Goodwood, Tam thought cynically, remembering regretfully that he had a mound of paperwork waiting for him to do back in chambers, even if the proceedings did finish early that day.

'Perhaps you would work out the arrangements between you... representatives of the solicitors from both sides to be there, of course, counsel too if you wish. I see no need for anybody to be there from the court... and I shall be very interested to hear about it all tomorrow...'

The next morning, Tam was sitting outside Court 51 soon after 9.30am looking at photographs of two sturdy looking houses of the modern style. Quite attractive, he thought and spacious for the modern day and age in which we lived. The photographs, taken the evening before, showed three areas on each house, first where the plaster fascia was intact but showing fierce-looking cracks, and then again the same areas after the fascia had been removed for several feet...

Then Tam looked up and saw Harry Wolf arriving with his attendant throng of solicitors, the Kingston Construction Director and, of course, Mr Armstrong. But they were deep in conversation and Tam had no chance of even the briefest word before the usher poked his head round the door of the court to say that the judge was about to come into court. So everyone hurried in and took their seats, to rise almost immediately as Elfyn David came sweeping into his court and everyone exchanged the bows between Bench and Bar, that old world courtesy still demanded of the legal profession.

It often happens that on the day a case is expected to end, the familiar journalist who represents the Press Agency finds his way into court, so that he can see if there is anything in the result for him to report back to the newspapers for possible publication; and Tam noticed him slip into court and take his place on the row reserved for the press as everyone resumed his seat.

'Well, Mr Pearse?' enquired the judge.

But before Tam could say a word, Harry Wolf was on his feet.

'My Lord, having given this matter careful consideration overnight, the defendants have decided to take no further part in the matter, but to submit to judgement.'

'That will be for the amount claimed, together with interest from first demand to be calculated as laid down?'

'Yes, My Lord.'

'And your counter-claim to be dismissed with costs?'

'Yes, My Lord.'

'So be it,' said Elfyn David as he rose sweeping his gown about him, a fleeting smile upon his face. With a bit of luck, Tam thought cynically, he will be able to make the first race at Sandown Park.

Tam Pearse had never seen Harry Wolf look so discomforted, but gracious in defeat. He hurried over and warmly wrung his hand to congratulate him on a victory which he clearly had not thought was possible on Monday.

'Well, Mr Pearse, I told you we didn't need no expert witness, now didn't I?' said Bryan Murphy as all in the team congratulated themselves outside the court and before making off towards El Vino's, well known to the legal profession as the best place to celebrate victory or drown the sorrows of defeat after a legal battle.

Tam Pearse had to admit that Bryan Murphy had been right and he had been wrong... in the circumstances of that particular, rather unusual case.

Stranger on the Beach

Tam Pearse found that life as a barrister was full of interest. After all, any case that came to him would involve a dispute between at least two parties, who had been unable to resolve it themselves. It must have got to the stage that they had consulted solicitors, who had also been unable to resolve it, so that they had had to resort to litigation to ask the courts to decide the matter and had briefed counsel to appear for them in court. It meant that any case was bound to involve a knotty question which had not yet been capable of resolution: a puzzle which he would have to seek to solve in favour of his client to the satisfaction of the judge or the jury in question. But the life of a barrister can become very busy, as Tam himself found. The more successful he became, the harder he had to work because Challen, his clerk in chambers, insisted that he did, and, because of his own desire for fame and fortune, Tam agreed. It meant working sometimes late at night and occasional midnight journeys by train to Bodmin Road Station and then for Bodmin itself to be in time to attend the courts there in that busy Assize Court. All of this was counterbalanced by the generous periods of vacation which followed once 'term' ended. The long vacation of the High Court in the summer months lasted over two months, although of course cases still went on in the Magistrates' Courts, as well as the County Courts dealing with disputes involving lesser amounts.

Tam Pearse's best friend in chambers at 6 Damson Court was Matthew Lumsden. In the middle of one summer vacation, Matthew found himself basking contentedly on the beach at Sangenjo. The full heat of the sum was shielded from him by a colourful parasol he had hired from the attendant, who also looked after the small fleet of pedalos and half-a-dozen windsurfers. These were now crossing and re-crossing the considerable expanse of Atlantic, which was the Ria de Pontevedra just to the north of Vigo in Galicia, the north-west province of Spain. To his right, Margaret, ten years his wife, was anxious only to obtain a really golden tan and lay in the full heat of the sun, glistening under a coating of Ambre Solaire. Life in the law courts seemed very far away indeed.

'You really should be careful, darling, why not come under the shade?' Matthew suggested.

'Just let me do this side properly, then I'll put on my beach dress and we'll go up to the bar, and you can buy me a coffee and get the kids some ice creams.'

Lumsden fell back into his deckchair, rather old-fashioned like everything else in Sangenjo, and lapsed into a contented muse. What a good idea it had been to come! As a busy junior barrister, he had been more than a little apprehensive at the thought of being away for just over three weeks, but that is the way it had worked out. And, after all, it was the long vacation. Instead of a package tour surrounded by hundreds of other holidaymakers, all bound for the same hotel, at the same resort, by the same flight from Heathrow or Gatwick, he had decided to do his own thing. The idea had really started after the Easter break when the air traffic controllers over France had caused an exhausting and frustrating delay of four hours at Gatwick, to be followed by three hours more at Naples. The hotel at Positano had been very good but packed with English. To get away from all that, had been the thought. To travel by liner to Vigo in north-west Spain had been the solution.

Spending an hour in a shipping agent's in the City had produced the possibility that the Lumsden family might travel out to Vigo on the elderly Italian liner, *Ascania*, and return on the rather more glamorous French liner, *Antilles*, 23 days later. So, all that remained was to find somewhere equally unusual and out-of-the-way to stay. Prolonged study of Baedeker's Guide to north-west Spain had provided the answer. Sangenjo was described as 'an attractive small resort frequented mostly by the Spanish themselves who have holiday houses there'. It was, however, a small town and was shown to have two hotels, one modern outside and above the town, the other, the older Las Arenas, in the town itself, and close to the beach. Lumsden had chosen the Las Arenas and had not regretted it. It was presided over by the avuncular figure of Ramón Menendez el Padrón, who liked to be called Don el Piano because of his over-vaunted prowess at that instrument, which was a feature of his bar, and on which he could easily be persuaded to perform. The piano was not perfectly tuned, Señor el Piano was far from concert hall standard, but it was fun. It made for character. It was different.

Margaret Lumsden was more inclined to the orthodox in all things. She had been particularly suspicious of the Las Arenas because of the paucity of stars bestowed upon it in Baedeker. But it did have two, and luckily she had not appreciated that these were signs of a local, and not an international rating. She had been pleased to see that Lumsden had managed to obtain two rooms with integral bathrooms, although slightly put off when she had seen the decidedly ancient baths and fittings on arrival. But now, she was enjoying it all as much as he was. Or, perhaps, even more? Lumsden had just got to the stage on any holiday when, although still enjoying the rest and the sun and the food, he was getting a little restive mentally.

Now, he opened his eyes and glanced down the beach towards the sea.

Unlike the Mediterranean, the sea at Sangenjo had sizeable waves. It was the Atlantic, after all, and although they were not as large or as potentially menacing as the waves just along the coast in Portugal, where bathing was often dangerous, they were noticeable waves. Not too large, because of the shelter afforded by the Ria. But it meant that there was a perpetual enemy for a small boy to fight. Close to the incoming tide, Lumsden could see his elder boy, Luke, with a polyglot gang of children energetically digging. They were putting the final touches to a vast sand fortress to fight the tide. Language seemed to present no problem at all and, inevitably, Luke, aged eight, had assumed command of the allied forces. Most of these, he knew, came from the villas outside the town, occupied, as the guide had correctly forecast, by the families of wealthy Spanish from Madrid and beyond who had come for the summer season. It was a feature of the place to watch the Spanish nannies, with the prams containing the youngest in the families, foregather for a ritual gossip at six-thirty every evening on the quaint, little, stone-balustraded promenade above the beach. The nannies were all resplendent in uniform. Each seemed to be different, rather like a female version of the liveries of a bygone age. The colours of the dresses varied between the classic navy blue or black, to dark red or green or lighter blue. Each complete with white apron and a lot of lace. All of it was like something out of the past, mused Lumsden, but then Galicia was behind the times even by Spanish standards, perhaps fifty years behind? Or even more. The English had made the region fashionable in the Victorian and early Edwardian eras. They had built some of the villas and occupied the few hotels. It had been for them that the now antique plumbing had been installed. Then the coming wars had stopped the inflow of summer visitors, leaving it a pleasant backwater. It was on the way to becoming popular again, judging by the number of children on the beach.

Luke was obviously happy and needing no parental control. That left Mark, aged six, and Lumsden could now see him as well. He was sitting in the sand beside a couple of women just along the beach from the Lumsden camp with his large colourful beach ball. It was the pride of his life at the moment. The women had brought chairs onto the beach and seemed to have been captivated by the six-year-old. Perhaps this was not too surprising, because both the boys were exceptionally good-looking children, and six is a lovely age. As he watched, Lumsden's interest quickened. One of the women stood up. She was young, perhaps middle or late twenties. She wore a short, blue beach dress, which looked expensive. She was dark and she looked beautiful. At least, from a distance she seemed to be. Now he heard her laugh and she picked up the ball, throwing it towards him for Mark to run after. The other woman sat quietly in her chair reading. She was older, less elegantly dressed and turned out. Somehow, she did not have the appearance of a friend; perhaps she was some kind of companion for the elegant young woman in the light blue dress.

Mark picked up his ball and returned with it, not towards the family camp, but once more towards the two women. Lumsden glanced at his wife, but her eyes were shut. She might not approve of Mark being picked up by strangers. But on the other hand, they had the appearance of class and Margaret would approve of that. More important, Mark was happy, he was only twenty yards away and very much within sight and call. Lumsden sat back in his deckchair and glanced again at a copy of *The Times*, only 48 hours old and still not finished. Then, once more, he just lay back in self-satisfied contemplation of his holiday. One of the best parts of it so far had been the *Ascania*. Old and small by modern standards, she was now owned by an Italian line and had been travelling between Southampton and the West Indies. Hardly a rival for the *Canberra* or the *Queens*, but aping in every way the customs of the larger, more glamorous ships. There had been a captain's cocktail party for the first class passengers. And the Lumsdens were travelling first class. The difference in the price between first and cabin class had been small and it had seemed to be an affordable luxury. It had certainly meant a more amusing and pampered trip to Vigo, and it was a consolation to Margaret for the uncertain classification of the hotel they were to stay in.

'How about that coffee? Perhaps I've had enough sun for the moment.'

Margaret stood up, brushing sand off her body. She put on her beach dress and looked about her...

'There's no need to take Luke away from his friends, but you'd better go and collect Mark – it looks as if he is being a nuisance to those two women.'

Lumsden dutifully walked along the beach. The glamorous younger woman was building a tunnel with her hand underneath a primitive sandcastle, while Mark decorated the ramparts with pieces of stick to resemble cannon. She looked up as Lumsden approached and he found himself looking into a pair of very large eyes, light, sky-blue in colour and remarkable in intensity.

'I'm sorry if he's been a nuisance to you – but we are just going for a coffee up the beach, so I'll take him off your hands.'

'Oh, he's no trouble – we are good friends now, Mark and I.'

Her voice was low and charmingly modulated. Her English excellent with a very slight low accent. It did not sound like a Spanish accent – could she be French or even Greek? The very dark hair, now in a chignon, looked rather eastern Mediterranean. The ring on her finger which was not a wedding ring, and not on the engagement finger, Lumsden noted, looked very expensive indeed.

'I don't want coffee – can I stay with Tania?' interposed Mark.

Tania? Perhaps it was Antoinette?

126

'He can stay if you permit it – we have yet to finish this castle of conquistadors, as you see.'

'Well,' Lumsden hesitated. It would really be a lot more convenient than having a resentful Mark to cope with at the table, and after all, the small group would still be in view of the little beach bar. Tania gave him a charming smile. Her companion said not a word, but looked up now from her book and gave a faint smile as well.

'If you're quite sure he won't be a nuisance – we shall only be at the beach bar over there – if he gets too much, just give me a wave.'

Lumsden found himself looking into those quite startling, quite remarkably light blue eyes. Tania's regular features were those of a classic beauty, relieved by a very full mouth and transformed, as now, when she gave him a dazzling smile. Lumsden realised he had been staring and, a habit he had never overcome, found himself blushing.

'Well, see you soon – be good,' he said to Mark and turned away towards the beach bar. Margaret was already sitting down waiting for him.

'So, where's Mark?'

'Well, he seems to have found some friends who are building him a sandcastle, and he didn't want to come, so I said he could stay.'

Margaret examined the small group. The companion, as Matthew had come to think of her, was still sitting in her rather stilted fashion, reading her book, while Tania and Mark busily put the final touches to the sandcastle.

'They look very respectable,' said Margaret appreciatively. The air of elegance, the expensive beach chairs, carried an aura of reliability even at a little distance.

'We certainly don't have to worry about Luke.'

The first waves were swirling around the outer ramparts of Luke's much larger, more functional sea defences and he and his friends could be heard encouraging each other to still greater efforts as the sea approached.

Matthew, Mark, Luke – and John? thought Matthew as they drank their coffee. Well, perhaps they would have another child, and perhaps it would be another boy. It had not really been their intention to re-create the four evangelists in naming their children. It had just happened they had liked the names. And now? They were comfortably off. A convenient house in Hampstead made travel to The Temple and the Law Courts easy for Lumsden. A constant round of lunch parties and games of tennis with her many friends kept Margaret happy and busy, together with the tasks of keeping house and looking after two small children. Margaret had been working in an art gallery when they had met, and had never shown any inclination to return to the world of selling Monets, Renoirs, Sisleys and Boudins, a love of which had been their first common bond, and in whose works the gallery had specialised. They lived in a comfortable house in a sought-after district and had plenty of friends. It was all very conventional. Just a trifle dull? Lumsden banished the thought almost as soon as it formed. His practice at the Bar was varied and exciting. The common feature of all his cases, whether in the commercial court or the Old Bailey, was the infinite variety of personality and the many facets of human nature, that were revealed by the parties in any case of substance. And most of Lumsden's cases now were of substance. But, of course, it all meant hard work and late hours, and this break, longer than usual, was very welcome.

As they resumed their places on the beach, Margaret and Matthew saw that Mark and his new friend had completed their sandcastle. Down beside the sea, a chorus of excited howls marked the exciting and inevitable triumph of the sea over the older children's puny resistance to nature's rugged strength.

'I think it's about time we collected the kids and thought of lunch,' said Margaret.

Perhaps Margaret thought just a little bit too much of lunch. Certainly there would be some reason for a further class of keep fit when they returned to Hampstead. But a holiday is a holiday and time to relax.

'Thank you so much for looking after him,' said Lumsden to Mark's new friend as he collected him from her.

'You don't have to thank me. I have learned much about castle building and he is such a charming little boy – and so good-looking.'

Well, it could not be denied that Mark was all of that. But he was not the only one to be charming or good-looking, thought Lumsden. Standing beside her, he noticed an elusive perfume and felt a sense of awareness of her and even a quickening of his own pulse. But that was quite ridiculous. He was at least twelve years older than she was, he reminded himself. As he glanced up towards the companion, Lumsden thought he saw a look of disapproval, perhaps even of faint alarm in her eyes. It made him think, just for a moment, that perhaps it was not quite so ridiculous after all. But only for a moment. He had been a faithful husband throughout his marriage and the possibilities for dalliance, whilst on family holiday, would be non-existent even if he had not. 'Thank you again,' he said as he turned away and was rewarded once more with a swift and delightful smile, which seemed to have in it just a hint of the mischievous. Had his silent admiration been a little too obvious?

The Lumsdens lunched outside Las Arenas that day. There were tables and chairs along the side of the white building, hotel was almost too grand a word for it, which was long and low and stood on the other side of the promenade facing the beach and the sea, and separated from the promenade by a low stone wall. It was the fiesta of Sant Juan Pelos, whose church stood in the little square above the

129

harbour. Yesterday, there had been a religious procession and today the town was celebrating with a carnival. There were roundabouts and the impedimenta of a small fair on the town quay, and tonight there would be fireworks. A splendid display, if the promises of Don el Piano were to be relied upon. It was all very small beer, of course, when compared with the internationally famous fiesta of Sant Jaume in three days' time at Santiago de Compostela, just over 90 kilometres away. The local papers had been full of it because this year it was to feature on TV1, the main Spanish television channel. Lumsden had set his heart on going, but Margaret had demurred. Now he raised the point again.

'It's the chance of a lifetime, darling, and you'd always regret it if you missed it.'

'I shouldn't miss it a bit, and I'm perfectly happy here, and so are the boys. Anyway, you haven't booked any accommodation and we'd have to be away a couple of nights. Think of the expense when you'd have to pay for the rooms here as well. But you could go on your own, if you like.' The expense was a point, and so was the lack of accommodation, but, of course, he could always find somewhere just for himself and the prospect of roughing it a bit was a small deterrent compared with the experience of a full-blooded fiesta with, as the glossy brochures reminded him, the procession of the sacred relics of the Apostle. Many hundreds of years ago, his shipwrecked body had miraculously appeared to the Bishop of Santiago in a dream. On waking the bishop had gone to the spot on the nearby coast which had appeared to him in the dream, and there was the body of the saint lying on the rocks. He had brought it to the shrine in which it now rested in the cathedral. 'Pilgrims are now able to kiss the robe set upon the seated statue of Sant Jaume in its baroque shrine.' Well, Lumsden thought, he might not go quite as far as that, but it would be unforgettable to see others doing so and to witness the procession starting from the Portico de la Gloria, the masterpiece of Mateo and built in

AD 1217. It would mean that Lumsden would have to spend several hours on a local bus, but again this would mean getting a close look at the local pilgrims going to Santiago. Lumsden was a romantic at heart, and this holiday, so far from the beaten track, had woken some dormant aspirations. Perhaps he would write about it all when back in England. Ernest Hemingway had written with such understanding of the Spanish people and their way of life and had always been a favourite of his. Who knows? Perhaps he would emulate him. In any event, it was decided by Lumsden and Margaret that he should go, and his family would prefer to stay.

Just then, they heard the banging of drums and wailing of flutes and saw the Santiago carnival procession approaching along the promenade. It consisted of twenty or thirty revellers, dressed in costume as clowns or in Galician folk dress, preceded by some drums, flautists, a trombonist and a trumpeter, followed by a crowd of locals of all ages and in every state of excitement. The costumes showed signs of many years' use. Some of the floats were perhaps just a little on the tawdry side, but everyone was having a lot of fun.

'If Santiago is anything like this, I shan't be missing a lot,' said Margaret.

'But, of course, Santiago will be much larger, much grander altogether. The religious procession alone lasts all of one evening.'

'Well, don't get drunk, and don't get your pocket picked.'

'No, of course not, darling. When have I ever got drunk?' Margaret preserved a diplomatic silence.

That afternoon, Margaret preferred to read her book on the terrace, while Lumsden took the boys back to the beach. For a time, it was dull for them as the Spanish children had their siesta and there was no one to play with. Lumsden set himself up under his beach umbrella and tried to settle down

131

to his own book. In spite of himself, he kept glancing towards the spot where Tania and her friend had been. But it was quite empty. Gradually Luke's friends of the morning reappeared and set off down the beach. To his great delight, Mark was included and so Matthew had an untroubled afternoon. But it passed without sight of the beautiful stranger and, was it for that reason? not quite so pleasant as the morning session. On the way back to the hotel with the boys, however, his eye was struck by a very low, very smart, light blue Mercedes 380 SL sports car, driven by Tania herself with her companion sitting demurely and just a little incongruously by her side. Taking her hand off the wheel, Tania gave a cheery wave before disappearing in the direction of the better-class villas at the end of the Mola.

Social life in Sangenjo centred upon the yacht club. Lumsden and Margaret had had several lunches there, and had been struck by the way the Spanish wives congregated in a circle and drank coffee at one end of the pleasant club room, while the men stood round the bar at the other. Not being able to converse in Spanish, Margaret joined Lumsden at the bar and they had struck up an acquaintance with a couple of young Spaniards. Well-to-do and charming, they spoke excellent English and had invited them out on their ten-metre yacht. Luke and Mark had been ecstatic. It meant a return of hospitality that night at the Las Arenas. Lumsden felt that his Spanish friends, Carlos and Pepe, were used to better things, but at least the food was good. Don el Piano seemed to be impressed by the company the Lumsdens were keeping and needed some persuasion before taking his seat at his beloved piano after dinner.

On his way to the beach on the Thursday morning, Lumsden made a diversion to the town and managed to book a single seat on the local bus that would take him next morning to Santiago. It was a great relief to him that he had, because Maria, in reception at the hotel, had been pessimistic of his chances of doing so, and he had decided against the

132

expense of a hired car just for himself. On the beach, all was the same. The others, who had gone on, had lost no time. Margaret was 'doing her back', which meant lying on her tummy with the straps of her swimsuit pulled down. 'Oil me, will you, darling?' she said.

As he did so, Lumsden could see Luke in the distance, but there was no sign of Mark.

'Where has Mark got to?' he asked.

'Oh, he's a very lucky boy, he's gone off for a drive with his friend Tania in her lovely car. She seemed so nice, and very respectable, that I agreed when she asked my permission. Mark was left out of the gang this morning so it was providential.'

'Well, I really don't like Mark going off with strangers like that,' Matthew heard himself saying, 'but they certainly don't look like villains, those two. Who do you think they could be?'

'I think I've seen her photograph in one of the fashion magazines – at Ascot, I think it was. And her dress is certainly by Chanel, and that means very expensive indeed. I wish I could afford Chanel.'

In fact, Margaret spent far too much on clothes as it was, in Matthew's opinion. It was a subject they did not entirely agree upon. But just then, he saw Mark and the beautiful stranger coming down the beach.

'It can go very fast, that car,' said Mark as he joined them.

'Well, I hope you didn't go very fast on these roads.' Margaret was disapproving.

'Tania says she'll buy me an ice cream.'

'Really, you can't let perfect strangers buy the children things, Matthew, you'd better do something about it.'

133

So he walked along the beach thinking that Mark would stay with his mother but, of course, he did not. He had not previously really noticed the companion, but there she was, sitting in one of the rather surprisingly grand beach chairs. Lumsden was interested to see that Tania herself had now taken off her beach dress and was sunning herself in a bikini. Somehow she had seemed just a little too correct for the beach in her couture clothes. The bikini was probably couture as well, he thought, but there was certainly nothing correct about it. A bikini is a bikini.

Tania rolled over and looked up at him on her elbow, and he found himself blushing again.

'It was very kind of you to take Mark for a run in your car.– thank you so much. And now you've kindly said you'll buy him an ice cream. But my wife thinks it would spoil his lunch.'

'And what do you think?' she smiled up at him and once more, he was struck by the amused and mischievous glint in the lovely, light blue eyes, 'or does your wife really think that Mark should not be taking ice creams from strange ladies?'

It was so exactly what Margaret did think that Matthew could only blush once more. 'Don't worry, we are not here for much longer, my friend and I. But he is a lovely little boy, and I shall miss him.'

'Well, thank you again, we'll – I mean, he will miss you too, I'm sure.'

Matthew returned to his place on the beach, but found it more difficult to concentrate on his book, while anointing Margaret's legs with sun cream seemed an almost automatic task. Perhaps it was just as well that Tania was moving on. In any event, he was off to Santiago de Compostela for his two nights away in the morning. At the end of the following week, they were all due to move into Vigo for a night, prior to boarding the *Antilles* on the Saturday. When the Lumsdens

134

moved off the beach for lunch, Tania and her companion had already gone and Lumsden had a premonition he would not see them on the beach that afternoon, and in fact, there was no sign of them.

Next morning, the local bus was due to leave the piazza of Sangenjo at 10.00am. At ten minutes past the hour, there was no sign of it. Lumsden was sitting on a low stone wall with at least twenty other would-be passengers of every variety and description, but they all looked Spanish and local Spanish of the poorer sort, although they included some priests he had seen in the procession carrying the religious banners on Sunday. It was already very hot and the road was dusty. The prospect of sitting in a crowded bus for the next three hours or more was not alluring, but Lumsden reminded himself of the glories he would soon be witnessing.

At last there was the sound of an approaching engine and the waiting crowd picked up their bundles expectantly. But it was not the noisy sound of the local bus, but an aristocratic growl and to his surprise the Mercedes sports car came round the corner, the light blue of its coachwork glinting in the sun. And then it stopped. Had she chosen the car to match the colour of her eyes? Almost certainly, thought Lumsden as he found himself gazing into them. Tania had stopped opposite him, to the obvious great interest of the crowd of waiting passengers. The seat which might have been occupied by her companion was vacant.

'Mark said you were going into Santiago by bus, but I didn't believe it.'

At that moment, the bus in question came round the corner. It already seemed to be crowded almost to capacity as it came noisily to a halt.

'Well, it's full of local colour,' he said lamely.

'Local colour and local smells – if you can get on it at all – but I always go to the fiesta of Sant Jaume the Great if I can. May I offer you a lift as far as the city?'

Well, of course there was no refusal. Lumsden felt that he would have had to have had strong masochistic tendencies to have even thought of choosing the bus rather than the Mercedes, and he gratefully put his holdall in the boot beside a suitcase in Moroccan leather, also a rather impracticable pale blue in colour.

Tania was wearing a multi-coloured light jacket, over cotton trousers with zipped ankles, which looked quite like a pair recently bought by Margaret and now her pride and joy. Margaret would have been able to tell him, but he had to confess that, if they were the same, they didn't look quite like this when worn by Margaret. Driving coolly and efficiently, Tania was negotiating the winding suburbs of Sangenjo and they were soon outside the town and on the dusty road to Lambados on the coast where, Tania said, they should have lunch.

'You always go to the festival at Santiago, if you can?' asked Lumsden when the back streets were safely behind them.

'Yes, when I can. But for the past two years I could not go. My husband, he is ill and I would not leave him. Now he has made me come away for a rest with Maria. I have been quite worn out.' She looked neither worn out nor in any way a grieving wife, thought Lumsden uncharitably, and this was the first time he had heard of a husband, and surely she was not wearing a wedding ring? But now to his surprise he noticed that there was a thin platinum band on the second finger of her left hand, beside a handsome diamond ring.

'Since we are so close to our house in Sangenjo, it is silly not to come – besides, I wish to pray to Saint Jaume in his own church in the Capilla del Cristo de Burgos.' She turned to glance at him for a moment and, as always, he felt a positive thrill of pleasure in looking into her eyes. Did they wear a pious look now? He thought rather that he detected a look of amusement and success. She certainly looked much more like a naughty schoolgirl playing truant than a worn-down and worried wife thinking of prayer.

The journey to Santiago passed quickly. Lumsden himself was in a frenzy of emotions. He led a fairly prosaic and certainly conventional life. He had never been unfaithful. There was little time in a busy professional life for dalliance, even if that had been part of his nature. But it was not. So why did he not now feel disloyal to Margaret? Well, he realised that she would hardly be likely to approve of his being whisked off by the beautiful stranger in her luxurious car. But if she were to examine the facts and circumstances coolly, and to compare the discomforts of a crowded bus with the ease of the Mercedes car, he decided, she could logically do nothing but approve. Well, not logically.

As a skilled advocate, as they drove along, Lumsden tried to find out something more about his chauffeuse. But every question was parried. He had been only too ready to talk about his own career and found himself telling her about some of his more exciting cases. One in particular had been in all the papers: a mistress suing her elderly friend for promises unfulfilled and, as the court had found, unenforceable. Tania had read about it and Lumsden was pleased to think that his name might have been mentioned even in the Spanish newspapers. But had she read about it in the Spanish or some other paper? Was she Spanish? Where did she live when not in the holiday home in Sangenjo? She would answer none of these questions when he put them obliquely and when he asked directly, she would not even tell him her name.

'I'm sorry, but I think it is better you do not know too much about me. It is not discreet what I am doing in lifting you with my car. My name does not matter. What does matter is that I have saved you from a – what do you say? – a balling

137

journey in that bus. You should be very grateful to me and you should give me a nice dinner tonight in Santiago. That is to say, unless you go there to visit your mistress?' He assured her truthfully that he had no mistress and thought that she certainly had saved him from a boring journey. Her occasional lapses of English were charming and the origin of the very faint accent still eluded him.

'Well, I'd love to give you dinner – unless you think that that might be indiscreet?'

'I am being indiscreet already,' said Tania with the incisive tone of a judge who has pounced on the one weak point in counsel's argument. 'And besides, my husband's relatives will never know about it. Maria has a migraine and could not have come, even if I had wanted her.'

'And you did not want her?' Lumsden thought he noticed that Tania's neck and ears now showed the smallest blush.

'Maria does not travel well in this car. Also, she thinks that I drive too fast. But anyway, she had a migraine, so I was forced to come alone.'

'And what about all those people who saw you pick me up at the bus stop?' persisted Lumsden.

'And why should I not give a lift to a friend?' demanded Tania, as angrily as if she was being questioned by those relatives of her husband she had spoken of. 'Anyway, they are peasants.'

That disposed of that, and they drove on in companionable silence. That was the strange thing about her, thought Lumsden. He simply did not need to make any effort to talk. They seemed to have established an easy rapport. As if they had known each other for much longer. Almost as if they were brother and a younger sister – well, perhaps hardly that. Lumsden glanced down at her bosom, still heaving indignantly at the thought of being reported on by peasants – delightfully outlined by the thin material of her jacket.

It seemed all too soon that the signs to Santiago de Compostela showed that there were only a few more kilometres left of the journey, and Tania spoke again. He had told her that his first task would be to find somewhere to sleep that night, and now she said:

'You know, you are not a very clever man after all, or you would have booked before you came on this journey.'

'Well, I'll surely be able to find somewhere for just myself.'

'I'm not so sure. You must leave your baggage at my hotel when you go to look. Then you know where to come to take me out to dinner. Then, of course...' She paused. This time there was no mistaking the deep blush that started at her neck, spreading quite quickly to her ears and tingeing her cheeks. 'Of course,' she stopped again and then went on with a rush. 'Look, I have a suite booked at the Reyes Catolicos right in the Plaza del Obradoiro in the front of the cathedral. It is a former pilgrims' hostel, built by Ferdinand and Isabella of Spain in the XVth century, so it is very appropriate. There is a room for Maria. But now she will not be using it. It will be quite separate, of course, from me. Perhaps, if you can find nowhere, you could have that. But it would look bad for me if anyone found out. Of course, you are old enough to be my father, but people might not understand.'

Or understand too well, thought Lumsden. 'Of course, I could not do that,' he said, 'I'm sure to find somewhere.' But he spoke with more conviction than he felt or perhaps wanted to feel. 'Anyway, how old is your husband?' but she made no answer.

The Reyes Catolicos was a magnificent old-fashioned, but luxurious hotel in the Cathedral Square itself. They had had some difficulty in getting into the heart of the city because the streets were so crowded. It was fiesta indeed, and locals and tourists alike were out on the streets in great numbers. But, at last, they reached the hotel and parked the blue Mercedes in its large courtyard. Tania said something in a low voice to the receptionist, who seemed to be almost over-awed by Tania's arrival and immediately summoned the manager, who obviously knew and respected her very much, but looked at Lumsden with surprise. Tania broke into a stream of fluent Spanish and the surprise faded from the man's face. A porter immediately whipped all the baggage away and Tania produced her own monogrammed, slim gold pen to sign herself in.

'Now you must go and find your room. I will see you for dinner at 9.00 o'clock in the restaurant here. The food is very good.'

So Lumsden began his search for a room. The streets were even more crowded and he soon abandoned the list of hotels and pensions he had obtained from the Tourist Office in the square at Sangenjo. It was simply too difficult to find them, but easy enough to spot the signs of the numerous pensions and small hotels in the smaller streets running off the Calle de las Huertas. Did he really want to find anywhere when he had the offer of a comfortable room in a luxury hotel, and who knows what besides? But of course it was quite ridiculous to think that the lovely, young Tania, a married woman at that, had any thoughts for Lumsden other than casual friendship. Besides, she knew him to be married and with a family, and was obviously very far from being promiscuous; in fact, she had come to Santiago on some kind of mysterious pilgrimage of her own.

At first, Lumsden had nothing but refusals. Everywhere was full. When it was quite dark and after 8.00 o'clock, a small hotel in a rather cheap street admitted that they had a room for him. The Signor would have to understand that because of the fiesta, although he could have the room for two nights, he must pay for the first night in advance. Where

140

was his luggage, and would he produce his passport? Lumsden explained that his passport was in his grip and that was with a friend. He would bring it later. His explanation was accepted at once, as was the price of the room for the first night. He badly wanted a bath or shower and a change of clothes, but he had no clothes to change into. Lumsden hurried back through the crowded streets to the Reyes Catolicos. He remembered the manager had referred to 'Suite C' and had no need to enquire at the desk. The lift boy directed him and soon, with a slightly beating heart, he was knocking at Tania's door.

She was apparently all ready to go out, but agreed at once to let him use her bathroom and a dressing room beyond it to change into better clothes. Seeing her, very chic and figure-fitting dress, he put on a tie, and luckily he had packed an old blazer, so he would not let her down in the hotel Grill Room. But when he came out, Tania said, 'I've had a look at the menu for tonight, and I think it is better we go to El Retablo – it is all the rage, they tell me, and it is in the next street.' So out they went. The crowds were as thick as ever and now they parted to let some sort of procession through to the Cathedral Square. They watched transfixed, hemmed in by the crowd as the procession came by, led by a canopy under which an imposing-looking cleric was holding a velvet cushion on which appeared to be an old and shabby splinter of wood. A piece of the true cross? But Tania said it was the stave of St. Francis, left by the Saint after his pilgrimage to the city in AD 1098. Following more clergy, there was a column of hooded penitents, some in chains, others with rough crowns of very nasty-looking thorns. Lumsden had heard he would see the 'flagelantes', those who were scourged, and he noticed that some of the penitents did indeed hold nasty-looking whips, rather like the cat o' nine tails of Nelson's Navy, while others had streams of tears on their faces and blood on their backs.

There was all the movement, and all the noise and colour of a vast theatrical production. There was even the sound of a brass band playing heavy music. Could it possibly be the Dead March from 'Saul'? There was also the clang of bells from the cathedral, sounding out in solemn and deliberate tones as if announcing the swiftly approaching end of the world. And over all, in the enclosed and airless street, there was the scent of incense hanging oppressively about the long procession. It was all inspirational and Lumsden, not himself a Catholic, had the odd thought that although a stranger and religiously an outsider, he was being let into the mysteries of another order. He had a curious feeling that he was a part of it, and himself involved with the penitents in their endeavours to purge their souls in appeasement for the death of the Son of God. He was also reminded of a magnificent production of Verdi's 'Don Carlos' that he had seen at Covent Garden. The scene of the Auto da Fé when the Flemish hostages are burnt by the cruel Grand Inquisitor before the King of Spain. But that was play-acting, although it had been dramatically and gloriously done; this was reality. But then the last of the long procession moved away and they found themselves in front of the El Retablo.

The restaurant was in striking contrast to the scene outside. They were greeted deferentially by the head waiter. Lumsden spoke no Spanish, but again he thought that Tania was treated almost as if she were royalty. She certainly looked the part and had put on a pearl necklace of great simplicity but obvious value. The restaurant itself was one of the strangest he had been to, since it was situated in the middle of a vast antique shop and the furniture and decorations seemed more suited to a Spanish palace than a first-class restaurant. As he drew back a chair for Tania, Lumsden distinctly heard the waiter say 'por favor, altesa'. So Tania was an 'altesa' whatever that was. Your excellence? Or even your Highness? Dinner was a great success. Lunch on the way had been hurriedly snatched at the Parador at Lombardo's, but the dinner certainly made up for it. It was going to cost him a bomb. But when he asked for the bill, 'La cuenta, por favor' at least he knew in Spanish, the waiter looked blank and Tania put a finger to her lips. 'Do not worry, they will put it on my account – and I chose this place,' then seeing him frown she continued, 'but I will let you pay for my dinner tomorrow night if you want to ask me out again.' Well, of course, he did, so that would have to do.

On the way back to the Reyes Catolicos, Lumsden was struck by the great crescendo of noise in the Calle de Las Huertas. Fireworks were exploding in the sky and the same brass band was playing Valencia at considerable volume in the Plaza de España. As they approached the hotel, he noticed that Tania seemed embarrassed.

'Would you mind,' she said, 'I'm sorry to ask – but you know they do know me here. I mean, when you come up to collect your bag. It might look bad for me. Would you... would you mind walking up the stairs – not the lift?' Well, the bank of four grand, but ancient lifts were in full view of reception. But nobody used the stairs round the corner from them and feeling like a conspirator, Lumsden followed Tania up these with hurried and furtive steps.

Tania's suite seemed enormous. Besides a substantial entrance hall, there was a large sitting room equipped with a log fire and with several doors leading off. The evenings had been beginning to get cold in Sangenjo and it was colder here. 'Sit down a moment, and I'll get your bag. I put it in the bedroom for safety.' Tania opened another door and Lumsden caught a glimpse of a tester: a large four-poster bed with ornate, very Spanish draperies. The maids had turned it down and Lumsden thought he could see a pale blue nightdress, with lots of lace, draped over the side of the bed. Tania came in with the bag. 'So, what kind of a room did you find?' Lumsden confessed it was not too grand.

'And you've left nothing there?'

'No, only a deposit.'

143

'It would be silly for you to go there now – come and look at Maria's room instead.'

It was severe and functional, compared with the grandeur of the suite. But much more comfortable than his own rather rundown room in the small shabby hotel. It was approached from one of the doors of the suite, but had its own 'front door' as well.

'Look, I can lock this door,' said Tania practically, 'and then you would not be able to ravish me in the middle of the night – even if you wanted to – but of course, you agreed you were old enough to be my father.' Well, Lumsden was not old enough to be her father. He was forty-two and at the moment, he was not feeling a bit fatherly towards the enchanting young woman with the ravishing eyes, who was now smiling at him in a way he could only call mocking. Good-humoured, perhaps excited, but definitely mocking. But his own hotel was mean in comparison with this one. And it was far off. There were a hundred reasons for accepting what could only be a friendly offer.

So he did. And when Tania closed the door behind her, he heard the very definite click of the lock being turned. And just a very faint feminine giggle. Well, of course, he was pleased. And relieved. It would not have done at all to be anything else but chaste that night. It would not have been fair to Margaret. But well, yes, it was a bit disappointing. They had dined – and wined – very well indeed at the El Retablo and it seemed rather a shame that he should not have rounded off the evening with a goodnight kiss – in quite a fatherly way, of course. To be honest, as he put on his crumpled pyjamas, Lumsden could not remember ever being anything like as disappointed before. As he lay in bed, he could hear no sound at all from the other side of the communicating door. Or could he? Just for a moment he thought he heard a soft faint sound from the door. Or had he imagined it? In any event, sleep would not come and Lumsden got out of bed very quietly and with enormous

144

stealth approached the door and tried the lock. It opened. He could see the flickering of the log fire beyond. And then he heard a whispered voice from behind the door.

'Well, it would have been a poor compliment to me if you had not even tried the door.'

Tania was sitting in one of the high-backed chairs beside the fire. She looked quite adorable in the blue negligee with lots of frothy white lace. Her hair now hung down almost to the waist, the firelight striking soft reflections from its dark black coils. Or was it perhaps only very dark brown? It was difficult to tell. 'I think you'd better stop looking at me and we had better go to bed. We might catch cold.' She put out a hand and led him across the room and through the door into the bedroom, and pulled him after her into the vast depths of the four-poster bed. It was morally unjustifiable. It was quite disgraceful of him. But before he surrendered totally to the excitement of a long, long night something made him draw back and say:

'There is one thing.'

'Not your conscience troubling you?'

'No – but I have not got anything to put on. ...how about you?'

'No – do not worry. That is my problem. It is a good time of the month for me.'

Lumsden was woken from a dreamless sleep by a frantic tugging at his hair. 'Wake up, wake up, they've come to do the room already, but I sent them away – you must get out.'

He saw that the ornate drapes surrounding the bed had been drawn and that now the harsh sunlight of another day was shining strongly through the curtains of the window, cutting clean, hard lines across the floor. Remembering to collect his pyjamas from beside the bed, he hurried through the connecting door to the small room beyond where he

145

washed and shaved and dressed quickly. When he had done so, Tania opened the door.

'Now you must go and do your sightseeing – do not forget the Catafalque of Sant Jaume at the cathedral – I have other things to do – we meet at a new restaurant this evening, just as good, at 9.00 o'clock and you must pay. You will see I am going to be very expensive as a keeped woman for you – leave your baggage in the grip and I will hide it later on.' Before Lumsden could protest, she had gone, leaving in his hand a piece of paper on which he saw in clear and well-formed letters, 'Restaurante don Gaiferos, Rua Nova'. When had she written it? It looked like the clue to the next stage in a treasure hunt. Lumsden smiled at the idea of Tania being his or anyone's kept woman as he hurried down the back staircase and escaped from the hotel unseen.

The day passed interestingly and quickly enough. Apart from sightseeing, he saw another procession which was almost as noisy and magnificent as the one the night before. After it was all over, he found the restaurant quite easily and got there much too early. At least, he thought, he would now be able to find out Tania's full name. But no, a table had been booked for two at 9.00 o'clock certainly, but in the name of the Reyes Catolicos. Lumsden had to sit at it impatiently until Tania appeared. She was dressed in a completely new dress. How could she keep so many clothes in one small suitcase? She had put her hair back in a chignon, as he had first seen her on the beach, and was looking calm and remote, and almost uplifted on arrival. But Tania was soon questioning him about his every movement in the day.

The meal had been delicious. Whoever Tania got her recommendations from certainly knew his stuff. When they had finished the sweet, Tania looked at him quizzically. 'You were not much like a father to me last night. But I am so glad you like me,' and her long slim legs wrapped round one of his own under the dimly-lit restaurant table. 'I think we must go now. Quickly. I do not want any coffee. We must go at

146

'once.' And so they ran through the crowded streets as if they were in a race. Ran up the back stairs and into the suite, where the log fire was burning again. They did not get as far as the bedroom, but tore off their clothes in front of the fire. And then Lumsden remembered. With great difficulty, blushing and fumbling with his Spanish dictionary, he had managed to make a purchase from a *farmacia*. He did not quite trust Tania's assurances of the night before.

'I'd better use one of these,' he said.

'No, you do not do that!' Before he could protest, Tania snatched it from him and threw it on the fire. 'Do you really take me for a whore?' It was the first time he had seen her angry.

'Well, of course not, I only thought for you...'

'Do not think for me. Come here and do not be so silly. I can think too.'

Their second night together passed as gloriously and as passionately as the first, but next morning they had to start back for Sanjengo. Lumsden hid in the bathroom when breakfast was brought in on a tray. Breakfast for one, but luckily it included a large basket of ensaimadas, the Spanish equivalent of croissants, and assorted delicious Spanish bread with a large jug of coffee, which was quite enough for two. Feeling like a burglar, Lumsden slipped down the back stairs after breakfast. If anyone saw him they would surely believe he was a guest escaping and leaving his bill unpaid, but at least he could not be connected with Tania. Nobody saw him and he made good his escape, and was waiting in the Calle de las Huertas, just round the corner from the Plaza del Obradoiro, when Tania pulled up beside him in the Mercedes. In a moment his grip was on the tiny rear seat and they were on their way.

'You sounded more concerned about your husband's family finding us out than by the thought that Henri himself

147

might...?' he said when they had threaded their way through the narrow streets and were on the outskirts of the city.

'That is true. I was only 20 when I married Henri and he was much much older. And he is very, very wealthy and had been a widower for many years and had had no children. So all his money would go to his nephews, but then they thought he might have children by me. But then, for a time, he did not. Perhaps it was my fault, perhaps it was his. Who can say? Anyway, they thought I was marrying him for his money. That is a fortune seeker. But I was not.' She took her eyes off the road to look him in the face, to see if he believed her. 'I was better born than Henri – I was born in a very good family, and I was in love with him. You will not believe me, but I still am. He is very kind and now he is ill and I have been unfaithful, but Henri wanted me to come on this holiday. He wanted me to meet some young people. He knows he has not long to live and he wants me to have some friends later on...' Her eyes moistened.

'Besides, it is impossible, sometimes, to stop being raped... or do you say ravished?' It did not seem polite to suggest that the ravishing was at least mutual. It was not very tactful, but Lumsden found himself saying, 'Did you say your important prayers to Saint Jaume, as you wanted to?'

'Oh, yes, twice, but you know it was so difficult the second time.'

'Why was that?'

'Well, if I sin, I must pray to be forgiven, and I must repent and do some penance, and then I will be forgiven. But yesterday I had sinned with you and I thought I was going to do that again. And I did not repent. So that it was difficult to ask forgiveness. It made it better that Henri would understand or forgive me anyway.'

'Henri?'

'Yes, you see, he is much older. Because he is ill, he has not much thought for things like that. I think he knows that I have missed out. He says before I come away, "Now make some friends, I will not be with you always – you may need someone to be a friend for you." I think he will not be with me very long and I know you cannot be that sort of friend for me – so I do not know why I let you ravish me several times.'

She looked sad and Lumsden tried to divert her, but luckily, quite soon, they were outside the city and driving down from the hill on which it stands. The countryside was unusually green for Spain, in spite of the scorching sun of a lovely September day and Lumsden realised that this must be because it was watered by the two rivers between which they passed, the Sar and the Sarela. The bus would not have got him back until 4.00 o'clock, so they stopped once more for lunch at the Parador at Lambardo's. This time it was more leisurely, and neither wanted the meal to end. Conversation, at first brisk, became slower, the silences more long drawn out.

'What is the future for us?'

'There is no future, caro Matthew, you have a young wife, a young family. One day, they will make you an abuilito, what you say "grandfather"? I have a sick husband to look after while I can. Have no regrets and do not think I am too bad – if you think about me.' They looked at each other with misty eyes.

'You will never think about me at all.'

But they both knew that was not true. Suddenly the great adventure was all over. Tania stopped the car beside a deserted bus stop.

'You must wait for the bus here, it will not be long.' In fact, they had passed it a few minutes before.

'I must see you again,' said Lumsden.

'I do not think you ever will.'

'I must know your name, and where you live.'

'I cannot tell you.' There was a long moment of silence before Tania continued, 'But you know I did not mean that I should hurt you.'

'You have hurt me.'

'Yes, I know I have – and you have hurt me too, more than I would ever think was possible.' For a moment they looked at each other in silence, breathing slowly and then Tania leant across and kissed him on the cheek.

'Now you must go or the bus will come. It would not look good if I brought you back as well as taking you away from Sangenjo.' Quickly he opened the door and seized his grip, and almost before he could shut the door, the Mercedes roared away in a cloud of dust leaving him standing forlornly at the wayside.

The rest of the holiday was an anti-climax. Look as he might, Lumsden saw no more of Tania or Maria on the beach, and no more sign of the light blue Mercedes. Mark was back in favour with the older boys, and the long, lazy days of late September now had a decided chill in the evenings. Soon Lumsden and his family packed up and left the Las Arenas with many expressions of regret. And next day, they were waiting on the quay at Vigo for the *Antilles*, which was to take them home, with their luggage beside them. The shipping agent had told them that the liner was expected to be on time and that there would be a few other passengers joining at Vigo. These gradually appeared and almost to the minute, so too did the *Antilles*. First, as a tiny distant silhouette on the horizon which grew steadily in size.

'Well, it was certainly a most unusual holiday – I loved it and congratulations on organising it all for us, darling. My only regret is that I couldn't find somebody to look after the kids and come with you to Santiago de Compostela – I think I

150

would have enjoyed it particularly as you found such a good hotel.' Lumsden had told Margaret about the Reyes Catolicos. In fact, he had been slightly surprised that Margaret had been so understanding and had agreed so readily to his going off on his own for two days and nights. One of the young Spaniards, Carlos, had been very attentive to her and he had heard that on his first day away from Sangenjo, there had been a further trip on the yacht. If Lumsden had been a jealous man, he might even have been a little suspicious on hearing this. But he was not and it did not really occur to him that his wife might have been getting up to any of those things in his absence, which he himself had been in Santiago. It seemed right, almost fore-ordained, and he was suffering such pangs at the abrupt and final parting from Tania that he was surprised that it did not show, and even felt a slight resentment at Margaret for being so normal and unsuspecting.

'I'm sorry you missed it,' he lied, 'but you were quite right about the bus – it was very crowded – and very uncomfortable.'

Luke and Mark made no comment. For them, it had been a blissful interlude. The sea had been fought many times, and if it had always won, that did not mean that it should not be fought again next day. Spanish food was a bit strange, but the ice creams were good and they had been made much of by Don el Piano, whom they both adored. The voyage back to England on the better-appointed French vessel was as well-cushioned, well-fed and almost as entertaining as the trip out had been. The holiday drew to its close as the SS *Antilles* drew away from the quay at Vigo and the Lumsdens settled into their cabin, and prepared for their first dinner on board.

Work is a wonderful distraction for dramatic upsets of the heart and memories of Santiago de Compostela faded as the months passed. Of course, a separation from Margaret and the children would have been very upsetting, if not quite unthinkable. Of course, the events of a little more than 48

151

hours were not enough to have disrupted his life. And Tania had been so inextricably bound to the ailing Henri. But life was not the same for Lumsden. It never would be. As Tania had said, it was better that their parting was swift and was final. Better, perhaps, but Lumsden still had a very faint hope that somehow, somewhere, they might meet again, or at least that the mystery of a beautiful, rich, well-born, much younger woman throwing herself at his head should be explained to him. But, of course, they did not meet again, and the mystery was never explained.

Then one day, almost three years later, while visiting his dentist, Lumsden picked up an old copy of *Tatler*. On centre page there was a photograph of a group of people at the races at Bologna. In the middle of the group, looking straight at the camera with an expression of surprise, almost as if she would, in a moment, put her hand to her mouth, was Tania. Or was it Tania? Unusually for such a photograph, her head was slightly turned away and he felt a slight doubt. Was it only wishful thinking that he wanted, at last, to know who she was?

Lumsden read the caption: 'Antoini-Anna Georghiados, with friends the Duque and Duquesa de la Cruz, watching the line-up for the Calice d'Oro; see Jennifer's Diary page 32'. He had arrived early for his appointment and turned at once to the relevant part of the gossip column to read:

'Antoini-Anna Georghiados now has time to relax and laugh with her friends once more. Readers of the Greek press will already know of the trauma she has suffered over the last two years since the death of her husband, Aristotle, known to his friends as Henri Georghiados, the heir to the family shipping fortune. This was enmeshed in a complex trust under Greek law. Once Henri died, the fortune was to go to a number of nephews and nieces, with nothing for any surviving spouse. But if Henri left a child, the fortune would be that of any surviving spouse for life and thereafter to the child. Henri had no children by his first wife, Isobel, but

152

speculation grew when he remarried the beautiful Antoini-Anna, more than 40 years his junior, and closely connected with the Marquis de Padua on her father's side, and with the Duque de la Cruz, seen in our photograph, on her mother's. The months passed during the first seven years of their marriage with no pregnancy, but Antoini-Anna was still only 27. Even so, her relatives must have thought themselves safe, when it was reported in the columns of the Athens paparazzi that Hercules Georghiados was boasting that his own large expectation would soon be his and spending his expected inheritance, in advance, on the racecourses of Europe. And then, only months before Henri's death, on her return from a mystery absence, it was reported that his beautiful wife was indeed pregnant. Had she been to some fertility clinic? Rumours abounded, but the fact became clearer and clearer that pregnant she was; Henri boasted of his delight at the thought that, after all, he was about to have an heir. The reactions of his disappointed relations can only be guessed at, but it was accepted that they had ceased to have much contact with Henri and Antoini-Anna. And then, just after the birth of his son and heir, Henri died of a heart attack. The joy had proved too much? The thwarted family were left to fume and to draw in their horns in frustration. After a prolonged period of mourning, during which Antoini-Anna has not been seen, she has now emerged once more to retake the place in society which had seemed to be her natural right.'

Lumsden's feelings were agonising. Was this Tania at all? He knew that Antoini-Anna was a common enough name in Spain, and no doubt in Greece as well. It certainly looked like her, but a very different Tania from the one he had known on the beach at Sangenjo. Now haute couture and chic, then beach clothes and relaxed. Could he be sure at all? Did this provide the explanation and the compelling reason for the nights of ecstasy that he had spent in the Reyes Catolicos? Had he been a mere tool used to provide a continuing life of luxury for Antoini-Anna at the expense of all the nephews and nieces who were now destined to live in perpetual frustration that an old man, who had seemed to be far beyond it, had miraculously managed to impregnate his lovely wife? The episode had had a profound effect on Lumsden himself which, until his visit to the dentist that day, he had been managing to put behind him. Now he read and re-read the column again, but there were no more clues. No other names which he might have been able to contact to see if somehow or other he might find out more. There was no name given for the son, which could conceivably have provided him with some clue to help him to unravel what might, or might not have been behind it all.

Lumsden was (or was it that he only had once been?) a righteous young man who had had his flings in his early days as a student at Cambridge and as a young barrister, until he had met the very pretty young Margaret, herself a budding solicitor. And then there had been a whirlwind courtship and marriage, and the two young children. So life had been very full and very busy and there simply had never been any more serious affairs. He had been a very faithful husband and had never suspected that Margaret was anything but a very faithful wife. Until that excursion to Santiago de Compostela. And since then, he had been able to put it all behind him and continue the virtuous life he had previously led. He had half convinced himself that it had never happened at all. That he had had far too much to drink with the lovely stranger whose name even he did not know, and that the nights in bed had been only wishful thinking. How could they be anything else? he asked himself. After all, he was a respected married man and the stranger was an obviously well-connected married women. He was not even sure of her nationality. She spoke excellent Spanish, as was obvious, but had occasionally said to a waiter 'efharisto' instead of the 'gracias' or 'obrigad' he would have expected as the Spanish for 'thank you', and 'efharisto' was surely the Greek word for the same thing?

Of course, to him she had spoken nothing but her excellent English, with that faint and intriguing touch of an accent which could have been anything. The visit to Santiago was best forgotten. Lumsden had a lovely wife and family and was well-respected in his chosen profession. He would

154

one day 'take silk', become one of Her Majesty's counsel and probably get elevated to the Bench as a judge. He did not want to remember anything about his one fall from grace and after his visit to the dentist, the whole disgraceful... Yes, he now liked to think of it as disgraceful rather than wonderful, ecstatic, pre-ordained or all those other adjectives that he once used to describe the Santiago episode in his imagination. He had never confessed it to Margaret. It was the one thing that he knew that he dared not do. But was there any real excuse for it? He knew that it had certainly been sinful, and sins should be confessed and repented of for a hope of forgiveness. And yet he could not find it in him to repent of a wonderful experience which, as he now suspected after the visit to the dentist, had had a very good effect in the life of that lovely, unknown stranger on the beach at Sanjengo. Lumsden's suspicions were only turned into certainty some four years later when, once more, he was visiting the dentist. Once more, he picked up an issue of *Harpers & Queen,* and this time found himself looking at a photograph captioned, 'Antoini-Anna Georghiados and her son, Ionnis.'

The photograph showed a familiar-looking lady with light blue eyes standing beside a small boy, who also looked strangely familiar. In spite of the very different clothing and the unfamiliar ambiance, it surely might have been a photograph of Mark when Mark had been aged about six or seven? Matthew then remembered talking to Antoini-Anna about the four evangelists, Matthew, Mark, Luke and John, and the naming of his children, Mark and Luke, after them, with their hope, which had never been fulfilled, that there would be a fourth. His Greek was almost rudimentary, but surely Ionnis was their equivalent of John?

.